Grace

by Mary Casanova

For Capucine

Published by American Girl Publishing
Copyright © 2015 American Girl

Questions or comments? Call 1-800-845-0005, visit **americangirl.com**, or write to Customer Service, American Girl, 8400 Fairway Place, Middleton, WI 53562-0497.

Printed in China
15 16 17 18 19 20 21 22 LEO 13 12 11 10 9 8 7 6

Illustrations by Sarah Davis

Author photo credit, p. 196: James Hanson

Special thanks to Héloïse Blain, French teacher and language expert, Nice, France; Dawn Bowlus, director, Jacobson Institute for Youth Entrepreneurship at The University of Iowa; Dominique Dury, head chef, Flying Cook, Paris, France; and Donna Houle, special projects manager, Blackstone Valley Tourism Council.

Library of Congress Cataloging-in-Publication Data
Casanova, Mary.
Grace / by Mary Casanova ; illustrations by Sarah Davis.
    pages   cm
Summary: Nine-year-old Grace likes having a plan but she must find a way to be flexible and open to new ideas when she goes to Paris with her mother and has trouble getting along with her cousin, while at home her friends start the business she proposed without her.
ISBN 978-1-60958-891-5 (paperback) — ISBN 978-1-60958-895-3 (ebook)
[1. Cousins—Fiction. 2. Voyages and travels—Fiction. 3. Bakers and bakeries—Fiction. 4. Friendship—Fiction. 5. Paris (France)—Fiction. 6. France—Fiction.] I. Title.
PZ7.C266Gr 2015   [Fic]—dc23   2014040092

Contents

A Good Idea
Chapter 1

*I*n my pajamas, I raced downstairs and slid a few yards across the kitchen floor—just as Mom stepped through the back door.

"Whoa, Grace. Slow down!" Her face matched her bright pink running shirt. "It's only the first day of summer vacation. You have almost three months ahead to do all those things you want to do."

"But I just thought of a way to make Grandma's muffin recipe even *better*," I said.

"Ah, another good idea," said Mom as she bent to untie her running shoes. "You may use the oven, but can I get a 'good morning' first?"

"Oh, sorry. Good morning!" I said. "I'd hug you, but—" I blew her a kiss instead.

"I know. I'm sweaty, but I did seven miles this morning," Mom announced proudly. "It's only a couple of months till the half marathon." She sat down in front of the computer to log her progress, which she did after every run.

I am just like Mom that way. I like to have a plan.

I preheated the oven and then opened the fridge to pull out a blue ceramic bowl. Last night, I'd whipped up a thick batter with eggs, sugar, flour, and yogurt. Now I gently grated the rind of a lemon to make lemon zest—my new secret ingredient—and folded the zest in along with fresh blueberries. Then I spooned the batter into the muffin pan and turned to Mom.

"Can I bike with Maddy and Ella? We want to meet at the bakery for Grandma and Grandpa's anniversary celebration and then ride the bike trail."

Mom was setting out bowls, milk, granola, and bananas on the table. "As long as you stay within the boundaries we've discussed. And give Grandma and Grandpa a hug for me, okay? Thirty years in business is a long time!"

"I will," I promised as I put the pan in the oven and set the timer. I was anxious to see how Grandma's recipe—with my secret ingredient—would turn out!

While I waited, I took my turn on the computer in

the corner and checked my online calendar:

Today, June 17th

8:30	*Bake muffins*
10:00	*Help Grandma and Grandpa celebrate!*
11:00	*Ride bikes with Ella and Maddy*
3:00	*Go to library to check out books*

Then I took a brimming bowl of cereal to the deck outside, where I would still be able to hear the oven timer. A minute later, Mom joined me. Beside us, the azaleas bloomed deep purple, and somewhere high in the towering oak above, a robin sang its heart out. Then came a familiar *clink, clink, clink!*

I spotted Dad on the other side of the maple tree, tinkering with the ancient stone wall. "Hi, Dad!"

"Mornin', lovely ladies!" he called, peering over his shoulder.

"Fresh muffins soon," I promised him.

"Just say when," he said, and then went back to chinking out a broken stone. Our stone wall doesn't quite date back to the Industrial Revolution—when mill towns cropped up along the Blackstone River here in

Massachusetts—but pretty close. Besides cross-country skiing and building quirky birdhouses, fixing up that stone wall seems to be Dad's main hobby. It is a break from his therapist work, listening to people all day. But he once told me that stones whisper, too, if you listen closely.

Next door, the neighbor's golden retriever, Zulu, gave a friendly bark. I dashed over to the wall. She stood on her back legs to greet me, and I scratched her head and behind her ears. Then her owner, Mrs. Chatsworth, called for her, and she took off again.

When I sat back down with Mom and returned to my cereal, I said longingly, "Mom, can we please get a dog this summer?"

She laughed. "Oh, Grace. Before you know it, I'll be back teaching fifth-graders. You'll be starting fourth grade, which I can hardly believe. For a busy family like ours, a dog's a huge responsibility."

I groaned. "That's what I thought you'd say."

"It seems right now," she continued, "that you have the best of both worlds. You can give Zulu attention when you feel like it, without the daily work of taking care of her."

I was about to protest when the timer buzzed from the kitchen. "I'd better check the muffins," I said, hopping up.

"And I need a shower," Mom said. "What I do know," she added as she followed me inside, "is that you sure inherited the baking bug. You and your Aunt Sophie."

Aunt Sophie is Mom's younger sister. She went to Paris a few years ago to study pastry making and ended up marrying a French baker—and moving there for good.

"I love baking! I do," I agreed. "But I love dogs, too. And I can't wrap my arms around a muffin or a cookie."

Mom chuckled. "Good point." She reached for a hot pad and helped me pull a steaming muffin pan from the oven. The smell of those muffins pushed dog wishes from my mind. Did my secret ingredient make a difference? I couldn't wait to find out!

I parked my bike outside First Street Family Bakery

and stepped inside. Air warmed by ovens and scented with baked goods filled my nostrils. I breathed in deeply. Yum! I could live for a hundred years and never tire of that smell.

"There's my favorite girl!" Grandma said, beaming from behind the glass bakery counter, its racks filled with fresh cinnamon rolls, caramel rolls, doughnuts, and various breads. Faint country-western music played from the kitchen behind her.

Grandma shook her head of feathered gray hair. "You're coming at a perfect time. I haven't gotten the hang of this thing yet," she said, gesturing toward her new laptop. "Grandpa and I aren't exactly up to speed on technology."

"You'll get it, Grandma. It just takes practice."

She adjusted her red glasses and smiled. "Are you sure? You know what they say about old dogs."

I thought for a second. "Hard to teach an old dog new tricks?"

She grinned at me and nodded. "Now, what do you have there?"

I had almost forgotten about the paper lunch bag in my hand. "For you and Grandpa," I said, holding it out toward her. "Let me know what you think. Be honest."

Grandma peered into the bag and pulled out a lightly golden muffin. "Ah, you tried the muffin recipe!"

I nodded.

She took a bite, looked at the ceiling, and then smiled. "Mmm, it's wonderful! What did you add this time?"

"Lemon zest," I announced proudly. "I love getting recipes from you and playing around with them. It makes me feel like, well . . ." I struggled to put it into words.

"Like you're carrying on the family tradition?" Grandma offered.

I nodded. "Exactly."

"Someday," Grandma said with a wink, "you won't even need recipes. You'll come up with your own."

"Think so?"

"I know so. You're already experimenting with adding new ingredients. That's my Grace—always full of ideas."

Just then, Grandpa stepped through the kitchen's swinging door. His denim shirtsleeves were rolled up to his elbows, and in his big hands he carried a plate of assorted cookies. "Hey-ya, Grace! Come to help us celebrate?"

Today was First Street Family Bakery's anniversary. In the front window, a big banner read: "Celebrating 30 Years of Baking in Bentwick, Mass."

"Yes!" I told Grandpa. "What can I do to help?"

He handed me the tray. "You can offer a cookie to customers, if you'd like."

"Absolutely."

When the door opened and a white-haired couple stepped inside, they looked up at the bouquet of balloons on the counter.

"Thirty years," said the man with a wag of his head. "That's even before we moved here to Bentwick."

"Would you like a cookie?" I asked, holding out the plate.

He smiled, thanked me, and picked one.

"There are napkins on the counter," I said with a nod of my head toward the balloons.

"So many businesses come and go," the woman said to my grandparents, "but you two are still at it. That's really something!"

Grandpa nodded. "Well, we never gave up. We

started with just a few dollars. We rented at first, but eventually we bought this old brick building. Put in a lot of elbow grease to get it shipshape. It wasn't easy. Took a while to get used to getting up at three a.m., but I've never regretted it."

"We've sure met some wonderful customers," Grandma added. "It's fun to do what you love and share it with others. It makes for a good life." She linked arms with Grandpa and smiled at him.

As more customers strolled in, I offered them cookies, too. Grandpa usually works in the kitchen, but today he lingered by the counter with me, visiting with everyone.

In between customers, an idea that had crossed my mind before suddenly tumbled out of my mouth. "Someday, I want to start a business, just like you two."

For a moment my words—"start a business"—hung in the air like shirts on a clothesline. Clean and fresh.

Grandma and Grandpa shared a knowing look and a smile, as if they understood me perfectly. And then Grandpa said, "Well, why not? You get to be your own boss. You get an idea, and you can just run with it."

"That's the part that seems really fun!" I said. "Plus,

I love to find something that interests me and jump on the computer to learn more. I just wish I could do something right now."

Grandma reached for a copy of the *Boston Globe* behind the counter and started paging through it. "We just read something recently about kids who've started their own businesses . . ."

"Really? So maybe I don't have to wait to start something?" Excitement bubbled up in me like a carbonated drink. Shake it up and look out!

"Sure. You just have to come up with an idea that you can make work," Grandpa said.

"But what would I do?" I wondered aloud.

"Brainstorm," Grandpa said. "Keep your eyes and mind open, and you'll come up with something."

His confidence was contagious—in a good way.

I could do this. I really could!

A Change of Plans
Chapter 2

When the bell above the door jingled, I turned, expecting more customers. But instead, my friends stepped in, right on time. "Hi, Maddy! Hi, Ella!"

Red curls in a ponytail, Maddy bounced across the tiled floor and squeezed my waist. "First day of summer vacation! I'm so excited."

Ella hung back for a second by the door, and then she stepped forward and chimed in. "Hey, Grace!"

Ella has a look about her—deep bronze skin, thick black eyelashes, and the kind of hair you see in shampoo commercials. She could grow up to be a movie star, except that she's super shy—until you get to know her.

From outside the door came a deep *"Woof! Woof! Woof!"*

"Murphy," Ella said with a toss of her head that sent her long waves swooshing. "Sorry. He'll just keep barking, so I guess I'll go back outside."

"Do you want a cookie first?" I asked.

But Grandma held out a tray of glazed doughnuts instead. "Wait, go ahead and pick one. I know you girls love these. My treat."

I picked chocolate with coconut sprinkles. Maddy, I knew, would pick the cherry doughnut with pink frosting, and Ella, as always, went for the cinnamon-sprinkled doughnut.

With a chorus of thanks, we headed outside.

When Murphy spotted Ella's doughnut, his black nose twitched under a mass of shaggy gray. A medium-sized dog, he had come from the local animal shelter. When anyone asks about his breed, Ella just says, "He's a lovable mutt."

She handed him her last morsel, and Murphy took it softly from her fingers.

"He's such a good dog," I said. "You're lucky."

Ella patted Murphy's head and then unhooked his leash from the lamppost. "I have to walk him back home quick and get my bike."

As Maddy and I rode slowly alongside Ella and Murphy, I shared my latest idea about starting a business someday. "But my grandparents made me realize, why wait? I could start something *now*."

"Hey," Maddy said, her eyes shining with enthusiasm. "Why don't we start a business . . . together?"

I shot her a smile. "Oh, that would be so fun!"

"We could sell stuff online," Maddy said, starting to talk faster. I always know that when her words speed up, she's getting more and more excited. "I'm good at art and computer stuff. And these days, everybody's online."

"Even my grandparents," I said with a smile. "At least they're trying."

"I'm okay at math," Ella said, her voice just above a whisper, as she waited with Murphy at the light.

"You're *okay*?" I straddled my bike. "Ella Petronia, you were only the top of the third grade last year!"

Ella looked down, but the corners of her mouth turned upward. "Okay, I'm pretty good. If we start a business, I could handle numbers and money."

I wondered what I had to offer. Then I remembered my talk with Mom on the deck. "Hey, I love to bake," I said, feeling that fizzy energy bubbling up again. "Let's start with a bake sale!"

Maddy made a funny face. "But everybody does bake sales. There's too much competition. Plus, it sounds a lot like the lemonade stand you started last summer."

I shrugged. "I guess you're right. But fresh-squeezed lemons seemed worth trying."

"This time," Ella said, "we need to make more money than we spend."

I laughed. "Yes! That's the goal!"

When the light turned green, we headed toward Ella's house, which was about two blocks away.

"So, what else could we do?" I said. "Wash cars?"

Maddy rolled her eyes. "The high-schoolers always wash cars to raise money for something or other."

"Weed gardens?" I suggested. I pictured us leaning over flower and vegetable gardens all day. Hot, sweaty, dirt under our nails . . . I looked at my clean hands. "Ah, maybe not."

"Mow yards?" Maddy added.

"I have it!" Ella said. "We could tutor kids in math!"

"Um," Maddy said, as if considering it, "*you* could tutor kids in math. Not me."

We turned in at the white-fenced yard and green

A Change of Plans

two-story house with yellow trim. Ella put Murphy
in the house and retrieved her bike from the garage.
But the moment we started pedaling down the street
toward the bike trail, the chain on Ella's bike started to
squeal. *Schweek! Schweek!*

"Oh, it's so embarrassing," Ella said. "It sounds like
a parrot!"

Schweek! Schweek!

"A sick parrot!" Maddy laughed.

"A dying parrot!" I added, pulling to a stop. "But
I bet Josh can fix it."

We *schweeked* our way seven blocks to my house.
Like many mill houses near the river, the original
house is over a hundred and fifty years old, with newer
additions, like the garage. The garage door was open,
and what looked like a thousand bike pieces were
spread out on newspaper. Josh, my fourteen-year-old
brother, was definitely here somewhere.

Deep piano chords floated out from the living room
window, which meant he'd somehow gotten distracted
from his work on the bike.

"I'll go get him," I said.

I headed in through the garage, past the laundry

room, and into the living room, where Josh was playing our upright piano. I tapped his shoulder. "Hey, Josh," I said. "Can you take a look at Ella's bike?"

He played a few more chords, and then found a resting spot with his long fingers and stopped.

"Sure. What's wrong?" Dark hair fell across his eyes, and he pushed the strands back. My friends say my brother is really cute, but to me he's just Josh. I followed him back out to the garage, where my friends waited.

"It sounds terrible," Ella said.

"That bad, huh?" he said with a tilt of his head toward the house.

Ella blushed. "No, not the piano. That was nice."

"Her bike," Maddy said.

"I'll take a look," Josh said, rolling the bike into the garage.

As we waited in a patch of sunlight in the driveway, Ella said, "I'd like to ask for a new bike so I won't feel so embarrassed, but my parents will say no."

Maddy studied her bike, which was short with pink tassels on the handlebars. "And I'm tired of my little-kid's bike. I want a real bike!"

"Me, too," Ella said. "But my dad would say"—she deepened her voice—"'There's a difference, Ellie, between want and need.'"

"Then you know what?" Maddy said with a smile. "A new bike needs me!"

We laughed.

I didn't need a new bike, but a dog . . . I couldn't find anything wrong with wanting one. Someday.

When Josh silently rolled Ella's bike back onto the driveway, I couldn't believe it. No more squealing. Plus he'd wiped it down so that it glistened, almost like new. "You fixed it that fast? You're really good!"

"Oil." He held up an oil can. "It's out here anytime you need it."

"Thanks," I said.

Josh passed the bike to Ella. "No problem," he said. "But hey, if you want new bikes, just find ways to earn extra money. I make a few bucks fixing bikes for Cycle Sports."

"We're already starting our own business," I said, standing a little bit taller.

"A business?"

I nodded. "The three of us."

"What is it?"

I hesitated. "Well, we just have to come up with the right idea. But we have time. We have the whole summer ahead of us!"

Josh gave me that brotherly look that said he didn't quite believe me. Somehow, that made me more determined than ever as I hopped on my bike and followed my friends down the street.

Blackstone Valley at one time had miles of manmade canals near the Blackstone River, with towpaths running next to them so that horses could pull barges along the canals. Now those dirt towpaths are part of Mom's running route—and my favorite bike trail. This morning, Ella, Maddy, and I shared the trail with runners and walkers, many of them walking a dog or two.

"I know!" I piped up. "How about a dog-walking business? Do you see how many people walk their dogs here? I bet we'd have a lot of customers."

"That's a great idea, since I already have a dog to walk," Ella said. "Every single day."

"Exactly!" I said.

"And we wouldn't have to spend anything to get started," Ella said. I could see the math wheels of her brain turning. "We wouldn't have to buy leashes or food or dog-waste bags because people will already have what their dogs need."

"I'm liking it!" Maddy agreed. "We'd have to put up signs," she added, talking faster. "But I could help make them on the computer and print them out."

"We could start by posting signs along this trail," said Ella. "It sounds super easy."

"And really fun!" I joined in, excitement fizzing up inside me.

The more we talked, the more eager we were to get our dog-walking business launched. Before we reached the one-mile marker on the trail, we turned around and raced each other back to my house. It was time for online research!

Soon my friends and I were sitting at the computer in the corner of my kitchen, next to the bay window. With Mom's permission, we looked up *kids* and *business* and *dogs*. All kinds of ideas popped up.

Dog sitting.

Dog washing.

Dog grooming.

Dog training.

And no surprise: dog walking!

But just then, Mom stepped back into the kitchen and cleared her throat, her cell phone in hand. She was frowning. Had I done something wrong?

"I just got off the phone with Aunt Sophie," Mom explained slowly. "Her doctor says she needs to go on bed rest until the baby comes."

Bed rest? That sounded serious. "Is she going to be okay?" I asked.

Mom nodded. "I think she is. But she's going to need a lot of help around the house and at her bakery. I'm almost wondering if I should go be with her." Mom paused, and then a smile crept across her face. "And maybe you could come, too, Grace, to help out and keep your cousin Sylvie company."

Sylvie is Aunt Sophie's stepdaughter. I had only met her once, at Aunt Sophie's wedding in Boston a couple of years ago, and I couldn't remember very much about her. I tried to picture her face . . .

"Paris?" said Maddy, interrupting my thoughts.

"You get to go to Paris?"

That's when it hit me. I was going to France? I was too dumb-struck to know what to say.

"We'll have to talk to Dad first," Mom added, "because it's a long time to be away—I'm thinking about five weeks."

"Wow," Ella said quietly. "That's like half the summer."

Mom glanced at Ella, and her expression softened. "I'm sorry to interrupt, girls," she said. "I know you were making plans together."

Plans? We'd just spent the whole morning working toward launching a business together! It was like flying along at high speed on a bike and hitting a wall. No, not a wall exactly. More like getting a flat tire. But Paris?

It was all so sudden. It changed everything.

"Grace," Mom said, "I can see you need a little time to get used to the idea. Let's talk about it later today, okay, hon? When your dad gets home. We won't be able to leave until we can get to Boston and have your passport rushed through, which could take a week or more. That will give us some time to plan and pack."

When Mom turned away toward the living room, I looked at Maddy and Ella and held up my hands.

"Paris?" Maddy said again. "That's so not fair! I would *love* to go to Paris for the summer."

"I didn't know you had a cousin there," said Ella. "How old is she?"

I tried to remember. "I think she's a year younger than we are. I only met her once, when I was like seven. I don't remember her all that well—we didn't have much time together."

"Is she nice?" Ella asked.

I shrugged. "I don't really know."

Maddy's eyebrows scrunched together. "What if she's not?"

I hesitated. "Then it could be a very long trip," I admitted.

"And what about our dog-walking plans?" Maddy asked.

I sighed. It felt as if I'd just ruined someone's birthday party. "You two will have to go ahead without me. I can join you when I get back."

Ella combed her fingers through her black hair, as if considering the pros and cons. "No, Grace. It wouldn't be the same without you. I'd rather wait."

"Yeah, me too," Maddy agreed. "Maybe when you get back."

I felt a wave of relief, and then a little bit of guilt, too. "I'm really sorry," I said.

Maddy laughed. "You're going to Paris! What's to feel sorry about?"

Bon Voyage!
Chapter 3

J like having time to plan ahead, like with last year's surprise party for Ms. Tureno, the world's best third-grade teacher. I started baking cupcakes two weeks ahead and freezing them. Then I invited friends over to help frost and decorate them with round pink, green, and orange candies.

Because the theme was "Happy Birthday to Our Star Teacher," I asked some students to cut stars out of construction paper. Then others taped them all over the desks and walls. When Ms. Tureno stepped into the classroom, she flipped on the lights and almost cried. It was a H-U-G-E success!

But Paris? How do you plan for going to another country? And for half the summer?

As I started researching Paris online, I began to get a little better handle on what to expect. And that's when I started to get excited. This is a trip lots of girls dream of! I printed out maps, information about popular tourist sites, and some French travel phrases that I could learn before the trip.

The more I thought about it, the more I couldn't wait to get to know my aunt's new stepdaughter—my new cousin—better. And yet . . . another part of me worried that no matter how nice Sylvie might be, I was going to miss hanging out with Maddy and Ella for five whole weeks.

To make myself feel better, I started writing a packing list. Mom came into the kitchen and looked over my shoulder. "You'll have to cut it down, Grace. One rolling suitcase each."

"But we're there for five weeks!"

"We don't want to be tripping over our luggage," she said. "We'll do laundry while we're there."

Mom had been to visit Aunt Sophie once before, so I had to trust her. I packed tennis shoes, sandals, shirts, shorts, and skirts. And then Mom and I drove an hour north to Boston to get my passport and to shop. Along with a travel guide, maps, and a French–English dictionary, we both looked for a few special outfits.

⌒ Grace ⌒

After a couple of hours of shopping, I gazed at my reflection in the dressing-room mirror of a small boutique. I almost didn't recognize myself in the pink beret and matching skirt with black bow. Leaning over, I smoothed out my T-shirt so that I could read the words printed beside the Eiffel Tower: *Paris Je T'aime.*

"It means 'Paris, I love you,' Mom said. "And it's perfectly lovely."

"And so *French*," I said, tilting my beret slightly on my head. Now I felt more excited than ever about the trip. I was ready!

A few days before leaving, we shared a going-away barbecue dinner with Grandma and Grandpa.

"Five weeks is a long time," Grandma said, her eyes getting watery.

"Just don't get any crazy ideas about living there. We've already 'lost' one daughter to Paris," Grandpa added with a smile.

It was hard to say good-bye that night. I was going to miss my grandparents so much! And then I started thinking about Josh and Dad, and my friends, too. As I stood by the window, watching Grandma and Grandpa's car pull away, I swallowed the lump in my throat.

The day before I left, I invited Maddy and Ella to a picnic near Bentwick Dam, which was just off Bridge Street. I didn't want my friends to forget me while I was away.

Under a hot sun, we spread out a blanket between the old stone mill and the river. I sat down and closed my eyes, listening to the water rushing by. Grandpa once told me that the Blackstone is the fastest flowing body of water in America next to Niagara Falls. I tried to memorize the sound. Would I miss it while I was in Paris?

I sighed and opened my eyes. Three kayaks made their way downstream below the dam, bright red against the sparkling water.

"They look like rubies," I said as I took my first bite of my peanut butter-honey sandwich.

"Yeah," Ella said. "Beautiful."

"Speaking of beautiful," said Maddy, turning to me,

"you're going to see so many amazing things in Paris. You're going to have to send us photos and e-mails!"

"Even better," I said. "I've been thinking of a way we can stay in touch and you can see Paris, too. A travel blog."

"Do you know how to do that?" Maddy asked.

"My mom uses a blog with her class. She already said she'd help me use her site. I'll let you know how to get onto it."

"Cool!" said Maddy.

"That makes me feel better, too," Ella said, juice box in hand. "I'm missing you already."

To prepare for the trip, I tried practicing a little French around the house.

"Bonjour, Monsieur Josh!" I said as I stepped into the living room. But the words came out all wrong and stiff-sounding.

Josh glanced up from the piano and laughed, but he kept playing without skipping a beat. "Keep practicing," he said.

His fingers found their way around those piano keys as easily as mine worked with ingredients in the kitchen. But unlike baking, trying to learn French felt impossible. "I know, I know," I said with a sigh.

"Hey, Grace," Josh said suddenly, resting his hands on the keys. "Take lots of pictures, okay?"

"I will," I promised, "but I wish you and Dad could come, too." My brother is sometimes a pain, but I had never been away from him for more than a week before.

He swiveled on the piano stool to face me. "It's okay," he said. "I'm trying to get lots of hours at Cycle Sports this summer. Besides, I heard from someone who went to Paris that the French aren't all that friendly." He grinned at me.

"Really?" My stomach clenched, but then I remembered something I'd read. "Wait, I'll be right back," I said as I headed down the hall toward my bedroom.

Armed with my travel book, I raced back to the living room, where Josh was now playing around with a new melody.

"Okay, here's what I found," I announced. "It says that Parisians are 'sticklers for politeness' and exchanging formal greetings—like *hello, good-bye,* and *thank you.*" I scanned the next paragraph and tried to summarize. "Americans, this book says, are so casual when it comes to manners that we can seem impolite to the Parisians."

Josh brushed his hair out of his eyes and looked up. "Huh."

"So it helps to start with a simple hello, or *bohn-zhoor.*" I struggled with the *zhoor* part. "Oh, and always say please, or *seel-voo-play.*" I made a face at my clunky-sounding pronunciation. Then I went on. "And always say thank you, or *mehr-see.*"

"Nice," Josh said. "They'll think you're fluent, for sure."

"At least I'm trying," I said in my own defense. "Plus," I continued, "they call men and boys *Monsieur,* women *Madame,* and girls like me"—I flashed him an exaggerated smile—"*Mademoiselle.*"

"So . . . it sounds like the French just have different ideas about manners than we do, *Mademoiselle,*" Josh said with a wink.

"Exactly, *Monsieur,*" I said politely. I closed my book, did a little curtsy, and then danced out of the room.

When June twenty-seventh finally arrived, Dad and Josh dropped us off at Boston's Logan International Airport. I'd been on a plane only once before, to visit Grandma and Grandpa Thomas in Sarasota, Florida, when I was three or four. I didn't remember very much about the trip, and honestly, the thought of leaving the ground and being way up in the sky made me a little nervous. I tried not to think about it as I watched Dad pull our luggage out of the trunk and set it on the curb.

"What will I do without you two?" he said, kissing Mom and then kneeling to look me in the eyes. "We'll have to video-chat once a week, or I'll surely perish from a broken heart."

"Dad, you're silly," I said.

But when tears budded at the edges of his blue eyes, a big lump of sadness leaped into my throat. I wouldn't see him or Josh for such a long, long time. I blinked back tears of my own and gave him my biggest hug.

When Dad stood up again, he squeezed my shoulders and said, "You have a wonderful time in Paris, Grace. And also, you take care of your mom while she tries to take care of everyone else. Deal?"

"Deal," I said.

While Dad and Mom hugged good-bye, Josh gave me two soft fist-bumps to my shoulder. "Have a blast, but make sure you come back soon," he said. "No staying there like Aunt Sophie did."

"Don't worry," I said. Then I wrapped my arms around him and pressed my face into his chest.

The little bit of French I'd been using at home must have rubbed off, because when Mom and I wheeled our suitcases away from the car, Dad and Josh sent us off with waves and *"Bon voyage!"*

"Au revoir!" I called back, before being swallowed up in the airport's revolving door.

I'd never seen so many people bustling around, headed to every corner of the earth. I wanted to know where everyone was going! But at the same time, I didn't want to get separated from Mom. I stuck close to her as we headed through the long security line.

When we reached the security guard, we showed her our passports and boarding passes. Then Mom removed her shoes and put them on the conveyor belt. From her shoulder bag, she removed her laptop and set it in a plastic bin on the conveyor belt.

I tried to follow Mom's lead. But as I removed my tablet and phone from my backpack, she shook her head. "No, those can stay in your bag."

"Shoes off?"

Again she shook her head. "Kids under twelve can keep them on. Just set your backpack in the bin, Grace."

So many rules! I worried I was going to make a mistake. My backpack disappeared down the belt into a screening system as another guard waved me to step forward through a freestanding doorframe.

I glanced tentatively at Mom, who had just passed through it and stood on the other side, beside the guard, waiting for me.

"It's okay," she said. "Go ahead, Grace."

I stepped forward and put my hands overhead, the way the guard had shown me. As I stood still, something whirred around me, taking a quick X-ray. Then the guard motioned me toward him. "Step out."

Phew!

I joined Mom and picked up my backpack from the conveyor belt.

"Now all we have to do is find our gate and get on

our plane," she said, stepping back into her shoes and sliding her leather bag over her shoulder.

That's when it really started to sink in. I was going to Paris—on an airplane!

"Mom, I don't remember much about flying to Florida when I was little," I said as I hurried to keep up with her. "I remember pretzels. That's about it."

"That's because we flew at night," she said. "You slept most of that trip. I hope you'll sleep a bit on this one, too. It's a seven-hour flight!" She reached over and tousled my hair.

But I didn't want to sleep. I wanted to remember every moment.

With a roar of engines and an amazing sense of power, we sped down the runway. I gazed out my window as we lifted, lifted, lifted . . . into the air! The runway sprawled below us, and planes, service trucks, and buildings stretched and then shrank as we lifted higher. Pressed back into my seat by the steep upward climb, I squeezed Mom's hand. "This is amazing!"

❧ Bon Voyage! ❧

From so high up, the city of Boston seemed to spread out forever. With Mom's help, I spotted the John Hancock Tower and the steeple of the Old North Church. The harbor gradually shrank to the size of a puddle, and still we kept climbing through a mountain of white. We were *in* the clouds!

When the plane leveled out, I looked down on puffy cotton balls, lit golden by the sun. I felt as if I were dreaming. I couldn't look away!

Eventually, lulled by the hum of the engine, I settled back in my seat. As I studied my French phrases, I felt as if I were cramming for a test. I'd be in Paris soon, and I had to be ready.

Time passed and daylight faded to darkness.

When the steward came by with a platter of rolled washcloths and, using a pair of tongs, handed one to each of us, I looked at Mom in confusion.

"For freshening up before dinner, I think," she said with a shrug.

Hot, steamy, and lemon-scented, the washcloth felt wonderful on my face and hands.

Next, we lowered the trays on the backs of the seats in front of us to eat dinner. I chose the chicken pasta, and when the steward placed it on my tray, I saw that everything came wrapped separately or was tucked into the compartments of the plate: a dinner roll, a tossed salad, and a chocolate mousse dessert. Yum!

As soon as I was finished eating, Mom surprised me with a small velvet box. "For you," she said.

"Really?" It had to be a jewelry box. I snapped it open, and sure enough, there was a pretty bracelet made up of silver links with a little silver bow.

"A charm bracelet," Mom explained. "I thought you might want to fill it with charms that remind you of moments and places from our trip."

I stared at the empty bracelet for a moment, trying to imagine the charms I might add to it and the experiences I would have over the next five weeks. Part of me wanted it all laid out before me like a road map, but of course, no matter how I tried to imagine my stay in Paris, there was no way I could know what was ahead of me. I would just have to find out.

I leaned across my seat and kissed Mom's cheek. "Thanks, Mom! I love it!"

She helped me fasten the bracelet to my wrist, and it fit perfectly.

Then I settled back to watch the movie that was playing on the screen overhead. Thanks to the vibrating lull of the plane, the warmth of the red blanket the steward gave me, and my full stomach, I fell into a deep sleep long before the movie ended.

"Grace, time to wake up." Mom gently nudged me.

I opened my eyes to sunshine as the plane dropped over countryside. But instead of the harbor and skyscrapers I'd seen when we took off from Boston, the plots of land below spiraled out from small towns like the spokes on a wheel.

Soon farmland gave way to greater numbers of buildings, and our plane cruised lower and lower. With a *thunk* of the landing wheels and the *roar* of the engine, we touched down on the runway of the Charles de Gaulle Airport.

"Ladies and gentlemen," the steward said. "Welcome to Paris, France. The local time is eight-thirty a.m." Then he repeated the announcement in French.

"Eight-thirty?" I felt half asleep. Was I dreaming?

~ Grace ~

"We're six hours ahead here," Mom explained. "It's two-thirty in the morning at home."

"Weird." No wonder I felt tired!

We followed the other passengers off the plane and down a long tunnel, and then took our place in a winding line inside the terminal. I reached into my backpack for my cell phone. Mom had already turned off the phone's calling ability, since it would be way too expensive to make phone calls home from France. But I could still use my phone for taking photos. We were in Paris. Better start getting photos for my travel blog!

"*Arrêtez-vous!* No cameras! No phones!" A uniformed woman with a French accent and a pinched forehead swept down on me.

My heart dropped to my shoes.

She wagged her finger at the nearby sign. "We do not allow in this area."

I lowered my gaze. "I'm sorry."

A passenger behind us whispered, "It's okay. You're not the first." He was dressed in a dark suit and tie, someone who probably traveled often for business.

"Thanks," I whispered back.

Then Mom put her arm around my shoulder and

said, "It's all good, Grace. We're in a new country now, and everything's going to be a little different. We just have to stay loose."

"Stay loose?" I repeated, glancing up at her.

"Sure," said Mom, demonstrating. Her arms became limp noodles and she gave them a shake. "Like when I'm running. If I'm too tense before the start of a race, I'll knot up and actually perform worse. Traveling in a new country is sort of the same thing." Then she shook out her legs, too, one at a time.

Mom looked so funny that I nearly laughed. But when I saw another passenger chuckling, I felt heat rise to my cheeks.

"Mom, stop," I pleaded. "We're in line."

She yawned. "Yes, I know that, Grace—a very long line. And I need to find creative ways to stay awake." She grinned at me.

I shook my head but couldn't help smiling—and yawning—back at her.

When we finally reached the front of the line, we made our way to the Plexiglas window where another officer sat waiting. *"Bonjour!"* he said. "Passports, please."

Mom pulled out our passports and answered a few questions about the purpose of our visit and how long we intended to stay. The officer studied her face for a long moment, as if making sure she was who she said she was. Then with an official stamp on the pages of each of our passports, he motioned us on.

"Here we go!" Mom said.

"Stay loose!" I said under my breath.

At baggage claim, we waited for our luggage to drop down the conveyor belt to the revolving metal track.

"That's mine!" I said.

Seconds later, Mom's luggage appeared, too.

From there, we wheeled our bags outside and hailed a taxi. Mom explained that Uncle Bernard and Aunt Sophie were very apologetic about not meeting us at the airport, but like many Parisians, they didn't own a car. Plus, with Aunt Sophie on bed rest and the bakery to run, it was difficult for either of them to get away.

⌒ Bon Voyage! ⌒

The taxi driver, a gray-haired man with deep crinkles around his eyes, exclaimed, *"Bonjour, Madame! Bonjour, Mademoiselle!"*

"Bonjour!" we replied. It felt weird to be saying hello to a real Parisian this time, rather than just practicing with Josh.

The taxi driver placed our luggage in the trunk and opened up the back door for us. As he sat back down behind the wheel, Mom leaned forward and showed him my aunt and uncle's address on a slip of paper. *"Parlez-vous anglais?"* she asked.

"Un peu," he said. "Very little."

"Can you take us to this address?"

"Oui, Madame!"

I watched out my window like a hawk. We merged into traffic onto the freeway, and at first things around us didn't seem so different. Industrial buildings. Billboards—in French. And a big blue IKEA store. But gradually, we traveled into the heart of Paris on ever-narrowing, tree-lined roads that wound past fountains, parks, and old buildings.

"L'Arc de Triomphe," the driver said, pointing in the distance to a massive stone arch at the center of a fan

of roads. What followed was some sort of long explanation in French, but I only understood one word: *Napoléon*, who I'd learned from Mom had ruled France after the French Revolution.

At every turn in the road, we saw people. They were strolling, bicycling, walking dogs of all sizes, painting at easels, resting on benches, boarding buses, and disappearing down stairs to subways. They wore dresses and suits, blazers and berets, scarves and skirts. They sat at outside café tables, drinking coffee and reading newspapers. They carried what Mom called *baguettes*, or long loaves of bread from bakeries, and drove the smallest cars I'd ever seen.

We crossed a wide and winding river. "The *Seine*," Mom said.

"Left Bank," the driver added. He pointed down the river to the symbol of Paris. I recognized it instantly, rising up toward thin white clouds.

"Mom! It's the Eiffel Tower!" I squeezed her hand. "We're really here!"

She smiled back. "We certainly are!"

At every corner, I spotted blue signs on the sides of buildings that started with *Rue de* this and *Rue de* that.

Rue in English? Easy. It must mean *street*.

At a corner, the driver pulled over. We were here!

Mom paid in *euros*, European money that she'd gotten in exchange for U.S. dollars at the airport, and—*voilà!*—there we were, with our driver setting our luggage on the sidewalk.

"Au revoir, Madame. Au revoir, Mademoiselle."

I mustered up my courage. *"Au revoir, Monsieur."* My words came out garbled, but the driver waved anyway and smiled as he climbed back into his taxi.

A flutter of wings went through me. We stood just yards away from a shop sign that read *La Pâtisserie.* The shop's front window case boasted a colorful assortment of bakery delights. Outside, customers lingered at a few small round tables and chairs.

"This is it, Grace!" Mom said happily. "We're finally here."

I wasn't sure I was ready. My shoulders and neck started to tense up. *Stay loose,* I told myself. *Ready or not!* Then I took a deep breath, pushed back my shoulders, and followed Mom toward the door of the shop.

Flowers on the Wall

Chapter 4

*T*he moment I stepped into the *pâtisserie*, I caught my breath. Colorful pastries, as beautiful as flowers, filled the glass cases. They were every size and shape—some garnished with chocolate and fresh fruit, others cut into wedges, circles, or triangles. Every item on every rack and shelf seemed perfectly made, as if to say "Look at me!"

"Bonjour, Mademoiselle," Mom said to the pretty dark-haired teenager behind the *pâtisserie* counter.

"Bonjour, Madame!" She studied us and then broke into a big smile. "Sister? Madame Sophie?"

"Oui," Mom said.

"And Grace?" she asked, with a nod to me.

"Yes! *Oui,*" I said, trying out a little French.

"Welcome! I am Colette." She grabbed a cell phone and stepped out from behind the counter, wearing a floral dress beneath a white apron. She tapped something on her phone, held it to her ear, and spoke rapidly in French.

"They are happy you come to Paris!" she said, covering her phone for a moment. Then she pointed out a door to the left, saying something more in French into the phone.

As Mom and I stepped through the side door leading to a narrow staircase, a chorus of voices greeted us from above. From the second floor, Sylvie smiled down at me, sandy curls framing her big eyes. She'd grown and changed some since the wedding, but I recognized her immediately.

From the entry behind us, Uncle Bernard—whose dark hair contrasted with his white baker's uniform— dashed up and insisted on carrying our luggage the rest of the way. "Please," he said. *"S'il vous plaît.* I insist!"

On the landing, he kissed me on the left cheek and then the right, and then did the same with Mom. Sylvie held back at first, but then she and Mom exchanged kisses on each cheek, too.

Then it was my turn.

"*Bonjour,* Sylvie!" I said.

"*Bonjour,* Grace," she replied shyly.

I didn't know quite which way to turn my head to kiss Sylvie's cheek and ended up bonking her nose, which she pressed her hand over. After that, she looked at me a little sideways.

Aunt Sophie met us at the door, her hand supporting her swollen belly.

"I thought you had to stay in bed!" I said, as Aunt Sophie bent toward me for an awkward hug.

"Most of the time, I do, Grace. But not every moment." She kissed the top of my head and looked me in the eyes. "I can't tell you how happy I am to have you and your mom here with us! Come in. I'll show you around."

"But first," Uncle Bernard said, with a nod to Sylvie, "we want to welcome you!"

Sylvie disappeared for just a moment and returned with her arms full of gifts. She handed Mom a bouquet of small red flowers and me a light blue bag labeled *La Pâtisserie.*

Inside, I saw a box of *macarons* and a *tarte* with a red heart at its center, packaged in a little red box. The treats were so beautiful that I almost couldn't imagine eating them.

"From your bakery—your *pâtisserie*?" I asked, amazed.

Uncle Bernard nodded and smiled.

Then I remembered my manners. *"Merci!"* I said, with a nod to my aunt, uncle, and Sylvie.

Uncle Bernard said something in French to Sylvie. She glanced downward and replied, *"Oui, Papa."*

"Sylvie can practice English with you," he said to me. "And you will learn more French here, yes?"

"Oui, Uncle Bernard," I said, pretty pleased with myself for already knowing at least a few French words.

Then Aunt Sophie showed us around the apartment, which looked as if it would take all of a half-minute. To the right, a kitchen and dining table. To the left, two upholstered chairs and a couch. A golden tabby cat lay resting on the back of the couch, but on seeing us, he arched his back, stretched out his front paws, and then sat tall as a statue, studying us.

"That's Napoléon," Aunt Sophie said.

"We heard about Napoléon on our ride here!" I said.

Aunt Sophie nodded. "I'm not surprised. Around Paris, there are lots of reminders of the French emperor, Napoléon Bonaparte. But *our* Napoléon rules around here."

The cat blinked slowly at Aunt Sophie, as if in wholehearted agreement.

Then we continued our tour. Off the hallway of the living room, the bathroom held a tub and shower, a sink, and a washer and dryer, but no toilet. The next door over, I saw just a toilet. At the end of the hall on the right was Aunt Sophie and Uncle Bernard's room, an empty bassinet waiting in the corner for the baby to come. And directly across the hall was Sylvie's room, with yellow curtains and images of flowers taped to every wall. But the room held just one twin bed. Yikes. Where was I going to sleep?

Aunt Sophie seemed to read my mind. She said to Mom, "You take that room so that you can have some privacy. The girls can stay in the living area."

Mom shook her head. "How will we send the girls to bed early so that we can stay up and visit? I'll take the couch. I insist."

"But I feel terrible—" Aunt Sophie protested.

"Sophie, listen to your big sis," Mom said, putting her arm around Aunt Sophie's shoulder.

Aunt Sophie sighed. "Do I have a choice? Once you've made up your mind . . ." She grinned and rested her head playfully on Mom's shoulder.

As I followed Sylvie into her room to unpack my things, I saw that she had emptied out a bottom drawer of her dresser for me, which was nice. She pulled a mattress out from beneath her bed for me to sleep on. And then she showed me my half of the closet, empty hangers waiting.

"Thank you!" I said, imagining the work it had taken to make space for another person in her small bedroom. And then I remembered my French. *"Merci!"*

Sylvie smiled, but she didn't say a word in return.

"I am happy to be here," I tried again, and then couldn't help gushing. "Thanks for letting me share your room, Sylvie. We barely had any time together when you came for the wedding. But now, we have weeks! We're going to have so much fun together!"

Sylvie nodded, smiling more faintly this time. And then, almost as if I weren't there, she sat down on her bed and opened a magazine. She reached for her scissors and began carefully cutting out a photo of yellow tulips. I swallowed my disappointment. I honestly didn't know how she felt about me showing up and sharing her room for five weeks.

Aunt Sophie peeked in on us. "Everything okay?" she asked me.

I smiled. "Yes."

She nodded at Sylvie and at the wall of artwork. "Sylvie's been busy making flower art ever since she lost her grandma. She says it cheers her up."

Sylvie looked up briefly and then went back to her work. I doubted she understood a word her American-born stepmother had said.

As I hung my clothes in the closet, Sylvie glanced at me now and then, but mostly she kept her eyes on what she was doing. When I was finished, she seemed to have finished her project, too—she had glued the tulip photos to a sheet of red construction paper and taped it on the wall above her bed.

"My friends and I like to make things like that sometimes, too," I said, trying again.

Sylvie glanced over her shoulder at me just as Napoléon sauntered into our room. He hopped up on the bed and eyed me as Sylvie cleaned up after her project. I reached up to pet him, but he promptly darted back out toward the hallway. Huh.

He wasn't going overboard trying to make me feel welcome either.

I was happy when Aunt Sophie called us into the kitchen for lunch. As we sat down, Uncle Bernard served up a plate of cold asparagus spears wrapped in strips of carrots. I glanced at Mom, wondering if this was it—our whole lunch.

Mom gave me a look that said I'd better grin and bear it.

As it turned out, lunch came in courses. Aunt Sophie explained that the first course is always vegetables or soup. Second course: roast chicken with French fries—yum! Last course: stewed apple with an assortment of cheeses. I wasn't sure about the apple at first, but when I tasted a bite, it melted in my mouth.

I finished each course quickly—I was hungry! But I noticed that Sylvie, Uncle Bernard, and Aunt Sophie took their time eating and visiting. I nibbled a bit more slowly on my cheese.

"The best thing for jet lag," Aunt Sophie advised,

"is to get outside under natural light. Fortunately, we live so close to the Luxembourg Gardens that we walk there every day. I thought Sylvie might show Grace the park this afternoon, and they can get to know each other better that way."

"Good thinking!" Mom said. "I'll stay here and clean up the dishes. And Sophie, you climb back into bed, okay?"

"Okay, okay," said Aunt Sophie. "But I never took orders from you very well, did I?"

They laughed and started talking about how when they were little, Mom always wanted to play school. She was the teacher, and Sophie got to play the student. "I never could live up to your expectations, though," Sophie said, grinning at Mom.

It was fun to see Mom and her sister joking around together. "Is that why you moved to Paris?" I asked Aunt Sophie, joining in. "To get away from your bossy big sister?"

Aunt Sophie laughed, but then she tucked her hair behind her ear and said more seriously, "I moved here because I love baking and all things French. I stayed because of Bernard." She squeezed her husband's hand

and then looked at my cousin. "And now with Sylvie, and another baby on the way, my heart is forever here."

Sylvie glanced up, hearing her name. She sure hadn't shown much interest in the conversation. I suddenly wondered just how much English she understood. Was she as in the dark about English as I was with French?

Sylvie and I approached the Luxembourg Gardens, or what Uncle Bernard called *Les jardins du Luxembourg*. We stepped through the steel gates, leaving behind the narrow winding streets and close-knit buildings near the *pâtisserie*. Inside the park, wide gravel pathways, plots of grass, and trees stretched out ahead. "This is beautiful," I said. "And it's in your own backyard!"

Sylvie looked at me and smiled, but I don't think she understood a word I said.

When we approached a cluster of pigeons in the path, Sylvie removed a chunk of bread from the pocket of her skirt. She broke off a piece, crumbled it between her hands, and tossed the crumbs to the birds. They flapped to the ground, cooing and pecking.

Sylvie smiled, watching them.

I took a deep breath and mustered up the courage to ask her what I'd been wondering ever since lunch. *"Parlez-vous anglais?"* I asked. "Do you speak English, Sylvie?"

Without meeting my eyes, she shook her head. *"Non."*

No? My stomach sank. Five weeks ahead, and Sylvie and I weren't going to be able to understand each other. How much fun was this going to be? My excitement about the trip fizzled.

Sylvie kept her eyes on the pigeons as they pecked away. I'd never really looked at pigeons up close before. One was a mottled purple-gray, another almost apricot, and another white with tan patches. But I didn't know enough French to comment on how unique each one was. Without sharing the same language, I felt so alone—and suddenly longed for my easy conversations with Ella and Maddy back home.

Not knowing what else to do, I took out my phone and snapped photos for my travel blog. At least when we returned to the apartment, I could communicate with my friends online.

When the pigeons finished their last crumbs and flew off, Sylvie led me to a large, round pool filled with sailboats that appeared to cross the pond all on their own. Then I noticed that some kids standing alongside the pool were using remote controls. Cool. I wanted to give it a try! But before I could even attempt sign language, Sylvie was moving on at a fast clip, as if she wanted to get this walk over with and get back home.

She led me past pedal-powered go-carts of every color. Kids raced one another up and down an expanse of gravel, under the canopy of trees.

We walked past a playground with all kinds of unusual climbing equipment. One structure resembled the Eiffel Tower, with bungee ropes for climbing toward its top. *Maddy would love that!* I thought to myself. She has no fear of heights and will climb just about anything.

But before I could dwell on that thought for too long, Sylvie led me onward—past a puppet theater, riding ponies, a carousel, and a few food stands. When we spun around to head back toward home, I felt the sudden weight of tiredness. My brain felt fuzzy. And then it hit me. At home, I'd still be asleep—or maybe just waking up.

Just then, along the inside wall of the park, I spotted a small black-and-white dog. It was crouched play-fully, its curved tail wagging in the air and its head and shoulders low to the ground. Then I saw what the dog saw—another dog on a leash in the distance.

"Look!" I said, perking right up. "The little dog wants to play."

Sylvie glanced at the dog, and her eyes widened in recognition. *"Bonjour, petite chienne!"* she called.

The dog—with a slightly scrunched-in nose, upright ears, and short legs—lifted its head in our direction.

"You know it?" I asked.

Sylvie walked closer, squatted down, and clapped her hands.

The dog wagged its tail and bounded over to Sylvie. It was a female with a black patch of fur, like a pirate's patch, around her left eye. Sylvie spoke sweetly to the little dog in French and patted her head. I snapped a photo. *Click!*

"Where is her owner?" I asked, but Sylvie didn't answer.

I looked for a collar. The dog wasn't wearing one.

I scanned our edge of the park, looking for the little dog's people. But no one seemed aware of her or what she was doing. She was dirty and thin. If she had owners, they weren't doing a good job of caring for her.

Sylvie pulled the remaining piece of bread from her pocket and placed it on the ground. The little dog approached cautiously, then snatched it and ran off a few feet, as if to savor the treat in privacy.

Sylvie waved good-bye—*"Au revoir, petite chienne!"*— and we continued on. As we walked, I pulled out my travel dictionary and looked up *petite chienne*. It meant *little dog*.

The little dog was a stray. I was sure of it.

As we walked, I kept looking over my shoulder. The stray began to follow us at a distance, but before we reached Sylvie's apartment, she was gone.

I wished we could help her. But I couldn't even talk with my cousin, let alone help a dog while I was in Paris. All I could do was wish her luck.

Poor *petite chienne*.

I suddenly felt an overwhelming need to put my head on a pillow. I felt out of sorts—disappointed that

Sylvie and I weren't exactly hitting it off, lonely for my friends back home, and very, very tired.

I blinked open my eyes, wondering where in the world I was. Images of flowers pasted on colorful construction paper decorated the walls. A narrow bookcase held titles all in French. Yellow curtains flapped softly against the screen window. Outside, cars hummed by.

The twin bed across from me was made, with a hot-pink pillow atop a comforter of swirling pinks and grays. Was it morning? Was Sylvie already up and gone? I glanced out the window at the late-afternoon sun. Slowly, I pieced it together. I'd fallen asleep after our walk and must have slept the afternoon away!

I pulled my comforter over my floor mattress and stepped out to the hallway. The door to Aunt Sophie's bedroom was open. Her feet were propped up on a pillow, and Mom sat in a chair beside her bed.

"There you are, sweetheart," Mom said. "I hated to wake you. You slept for four hours!"

I yawned. "My body doesn't know what time of day it is."

"I'm struggling to stay awake, too," she said.

"Where's Sylvie?" I asked.

Aunt Sophie put an extra pillow behind her head. "She's down in the bakery with her dad. She disappears there for hours at a time. Sometimes I wonder if she's a little uncomfortable with a baby on the way."

"But why?" I asked, sitting on the edge of the bed. "How could she not be excited about a new baby? *I'm* even excited about the baby!"

Aunt Sophie shrugged. "She's been through quite a bit of change in the past few years. She lost her mother when she was younger, and then her father remarried. Me. That makes me the stepmom. She lost her grandma recently. And a new baby means even more change for her." But then Aunt Sophie smiled. "I'm so glad for Sylvie's sake that you're here, Grace. I think it takes a bit of the focus off me and the baby. She can focus on having a little fun with you instead!"

I didn't know quite how to respond to that. "I'm not sure she's happy I'm here," I finally said quietly, staring at the bassinet.

"Just give her some time," said Mom reassuringly. "You two will be getting along great before you know it. Maybe you can teach each other new words in French and English. That would be fun, wouldn't it?"

"Maybe," I said, but what if Mom and Aunt Sophie were wrong? What if Sylvie and I didn't start getting along soon? Five weeks could be a very, very long visit. And all the while, Ella and Maddy would be hanging out back home, growing closer every day—while I grew more distant.

I left the room and headed to the kitchen for a glass of water. The refrigerator was covered with magnets and photos. There were photos of my aunt with Uncle Bernard, including a wedding photo with a zillion relatives. I looked closely and found myself wedged between my parents.

There were photos of Sylvie on her bike, Sylvie by a fountain, and Sylvie with the cat. I was used to having an older brother, so I never knew what it meant to get all the attention. Maybe Sylvie wondered how she'd fit into her family after the new baby came.

"Those are her grandparents," Mom said, coming up behind me. She pointed to a photo of an elderly couple. "Sylvie lost her grandmother a month ago. That's one reason your aunt asked for extra support. They'd been counting on Uncle Bernard's mother to be here to help out with the baby, and instead, they're all feeling the loss of her in their lives. But maybe that also explains why Sylvie is feeling blue. Aunt Sophie says that Sylvie and her grandmother were quite close."

"Oh" was all I could say. I tried to put myself in Sylvie's shoes. I couldn't imagine a day when I couldn't step into First Street Family Bakery and see Grandma, or play cards with her, or have one of our "tea parties" together. I'd feel lost, too. I felt sad for Sylvie, but still, I wished she could at least try to pretend to be happy that I was here.

I gazed out the window. Shadows fell across blue shutters and window boxes filled with red flowers.

Mom seemed to pick up on my mood. "Tell you what. Tomorrow morning, let's go see some sights together. We'll borrow bikes from Aunt Sophie and Sylvie and explore. How does that sound?"

The dark clouds hanging over my head parted instantly. "That would be great!" I said. "I can get photos for my travel blog. I really need to keep in touch with my friends." I paused. "But what about Aunt Sophie? Can you leave her?"

Aunt Sophie called from her bedroom. "I'm just a phone call away! I'll be fine!"

Just then the apartment door opened. *"Bonsoir,* Grace!" Uncle Bernard said. As Sylvie stepped in behind her dad, Napoléon leaped from the couch and wound his way around her ankles.

"Bonsoir, Uncle Bernard," I replied. *"Bonsoir,* Sylvie."

"Bonsoir, Grace," she replied softly.

"Avez-vous faim?" he asked.

I shrugged. I had no idea what he was asking, until he mimed eating.

"Oh. *Oui! J'ai faim."*

Uncle Bernard nodded his approval. "I hope you are hungry, Grace. Tonight, I cook."

"Yes," I said. "I'm very hungry!"

"And you, Sylvie? Will you be ready to eat?" he asked, placing his hand on Sylvie's shoulder.

"Oui, j'ai faim," she said. So she did understand some English!

But when I smiled at Sylvie, she glanced down at the floor.

∾ Flowers on the Wall ∾

∾

Before dinner, Mom helped me post my first few photos to my travel blog. Then I wrote some captions:

Having a great time with my cousin, Sylvie, and her cat, Napoléon, I lied.

First day at Luxembourg Gardens and saw this little dog (petite chienne) who needs a home!

When I checked my blog before bedtime, there were already two comments from Ella and Maddy:

Ella: *Really pretty. And what a cute dog!*

Maddy: *Lucky you!*

I felt a rush of happiness. But now what?

Sylvie was curled up on her bed, reading a book, so I opened one of my travel guides. Before going to sleep, I silently reviewed some French phrases, hoping I'd be able to learn enough to actually talk with Sylvie sometime soon.

An hour later, I was still wide awake. Would my body ever get used to being six hours ahead? It didn't help that Sylvie kept mumbling in her sleep from the bed beside me. She sounded like she was scolding someone.

I hoped it wasn't me.

Paris by Bike
Chapter 5

*T*he next morning, Mom and I headed straight for the *pâtisserie*. While we studied the display cases with the other customers, I snapped photos of all the assorted treats and their French labels. There was *crème brûlée* and *flan*. There were *napoléons* (that name again!), *éclairs au chocolat,* and *éclairs au café*. There were *madeleines, truffles, amandines, macarons,* and *tuiles*. And *tartes* filled with chocolate, raspberry, strawberry, and apple. I couldn't believe the variety! How could I possibly decide?

I closed my eyes and pointed. Then I opened my eyes to see what was just beyond my finger. When Colette asked for my order, I said, "The chocolate *éclair, s'il vous plaît.*"

Mom ordered two double-layer round cookies. "Pistachio *macarons,*" she explained, as we took a seat at one of the little round tables outside. "Not to be confused with macaroons, which are coconut cookies, these come in all kinds of colors and flavors. But they are *always*"—she took a bite, and forgot the rule about not talking while eating—"delicious!"

"Bet they can't beat an *éclair*," I said, still savoring my first bite of the chocolate-topped pastry with creamy filling.

"We'll just have to trade bites to find out," she said, smiling.

After a bite of Mom's cookie, I couldn't decide which I liked better: *éclairs* or *macarons*. I declared it a tie. They were both amazing.

When we'd finished eating, we headed off on the bikes we'd borrowed from Sylvie and Aunt Sophie. Armed with a backpack full of maps and my French–English dictionary, I had planned to take the lead. But the busy streets—full of cars, buses, scooters, and other cyclists—overwhelmed me. I followed behind Mom instead. I wasn't about to get lost in a foreign country.

"First stop," Mom said, "the Eiffel Tower."

My heart raced at the thought of seeing that famous monument up close.

Paris by Bike

To get there, we biked along the Seine. At first I felt stiff and nervous, almost as if I'd never been on a bike before. But the more I pedaled, the more relaxed I felt, and it all came back to me. Biking in Paris was the same as biking at home and, at the same time, totally different.

My legs found a rhythm.

My shoulders loosened.

My eyes adjusted, going from tunnel vision and seeing only what was directly in my path to seeing more of everything around me: families with strollers, small dogs and big dogs, statues and fountains, and pigeons taking flight.

Riverboats traveled up and down the Seine. Other boats were moored below us along the concrete river-walk, or *quai*.

Soon, ahead of us, the Eiffel Tower loomed larger than life, reminding me that I was such a long, long way from home. As we biked toward the tower, I saw quickly that its base was way bigger than I'd imagined. The New England Patriots could play a football game beneath it!

Languages and tourists from what seemed like

every country swirled around us as we locked up our bikes. Then we joined a line of people at the base of the tower and waited. After going through a security check, we climbed the stairs to the second story and then rode the glass elevator to the top.

The wind at the top of the tower was strong, blowing my hair sideways and whistling in my ears. I held on to the edge, almost dizzy with the height.

Below us, throngs of tiny people biked, walked, or sat on park benches. Almost as if I had pressed the minus symbol on a computer screen, the city "zoomed out" into an ever-widening frame of buildings and streets, monuments and neighborhoods. And we were high above it all.

Click! I took a photo of the world below.

Then I pulled out my travel guide. As Mom and I took turns reading about the tower, I glanced down at the Seine, winding its way through the city's center. I made mental notes about some of the fun things I might write later in my travel blog, such as:

• *The Eiffel Tower wasn't supposed to stay. It was built as a temporary exhibit for the 1889 World's Fair.*

- *It once almost became a giant heap of scrap metal, but its use as a radio antenna saved it. Thank goodness!*
- *Painters use three shades of brown to paint the tower, and it takes sixty tons of paint!*

With the city stretching out behind us, Mom and I asked a woman—another tourist—if she would take our photo.

"Of course, I take!" she said in what Mom told me later was a German accent.

Click!

Before we went back down the elevator, we stopped at the gift shop. I added a tiny charm of the Eiffel Tower to my bracelet, the perfect first adventure. I sighed happily. The rest of my trip stretched out before me like a dozen silver charms yet to be discovered.

Mom and I biked on, crossing a little bridge called the *Pont des Arts,* the Arts Bridge. On the railings and sides of the bridge, what looked like a billion padlocks were hanging. Gold locks, silver locks, pink locks.

Huge locks and tiny locks. It was crazy!

"Mom, I don't get it. What's with all the locks?" I asked, slowing down and straddling my bike.

"Well," she said as she pulled up alongside me, "couples started adding locks to the bridge as a symbol of their love. Paris, you know, is called the City of Lights, but it's also called the City of Love."

Around us, tourists snapped photos.

"Oh. So somebody started it and it just caught on?"

She shrugged. "I guess so."

An idea flickered across my mind. "Mom, you know how I mentioned how Ella and Maddy and I want to start a business?"

"Yeah?"

We gazed over the side of the bridge as a small boat motored beneath.

"Well," I said, "we thought we'd start a dog-walking business. I knew it was a good idea, but when I see this bridge—with all these locks everywhere—it just proves how one idea can really take off. I mean, even the gift shop at the top of the Eiffel Tower sold little locks. I didn't get why, until now."

"You're right, Grace," Mom said. "One idea can

really grow. What do people call it when an idea takes off online?"

I rolled my eyes. "Mom, quit being such a teacher. I know you know the answer already."

"Hmmm. It's on the tip of my tongue," she said with a smile.

"Viral?" I finally said.

"Yeah, that's it!" she said, as if she hadn't known. Then she pointed to my backpack. "Better get a photo of us here, yes?"

"I'm on it," I said.

I pulled out my phone and held it out in front of us, with the river as our backdrop. *Click!*

While Mom and I waited in line to tour the towering *Notre Dame* cathedral, long-necked stone creatures—*gargoyles*—looked down on us, their mouths wide open.

"Creepy," Mom said, gazing up. "What do you suppose they were thinking when they built those?"

This time, I was way ahead of her. Before falling

asleep last night, I'd done some research in our guide-
book. I explained that eight hundred years ago, Gothic
buildings didn't have rain gutters. So gargoyles were
built to spout rain away from the sides of the buildings.
"Plus," I added, "people believed gargoyles kept away
evil spirits. I'd think they'd just give you bad dreams!"

Mom smiled. "I agree."

"Wait. You knew all that already. You did your
teacher thing again, didn't you?"

"What?" She gave me a wide-eyed look and crossed
her arms. "Okay, maybe I do that sometimes," she said.
"But I don't know everything."

I snapped a photo of the gargoyles. Josh would like
them.

Click!

"Either way," I said, "they're creepy—and kind of
cool."

Inside, in the cathedral's shadows, rows of candles
flickered. Sweet incense lingered in the cool air, and
shafts of colored light filtered in through stained-glass
windows. It was easy to imagine how the author of
The Hunchback of Notre Dame had been inspired by this
place.

I reached for Mom's hand and whispered, "You know how Dad says stones talk, if you listen?"

"Yes," she whispered back.

"Well, I bet these stone walls could tell lots of stories."

"I was just thinking the same thing," she said. "Makes me miss him—and Josh."

"Me too," I whispered.

For lunch, we headed back along Boulevard St. Germain.

"Here we are," Mom said as we approached the café. Customers were seated outside the front entrance, and the sign overhead read *Café de Flore* in a pretty scroll.

"It's one of the most famous cafés in Paris," Mom said. "Many famous artists and writers have hung out here."

Customers sat clustered at green tables with pink-and-green chairs. Mom made her way toward an open table, and I followed, careful not to trip on some-one's purse or cane. As I sat down, my stomach gurgled noisily. I was hungry!

But when the waiter brought the menu, nothing looked familiar.

"Want some help?" Mom asked.

"I've got it." I had my French–English dictionary, and I wanted to prove that I could order for myself. Everything else had gone so well today. I'd seen the Eiffel Tower, and I'd even been inspired by the Pont des Arts bridge to keep going with my dog-walking business idea. I could certainly order my own lunch! All I really wanted was a grilled cheese sandwich, but as I scanned the menu, none of the words made sense.

When the waiter approached again, the menu blurred before my eyes. I decided to just put my finger on an item and order it. I said, *"S'il vous plaît,"* and then continued in terrible French, *"ragoût de lapin?"*

The waiter smiled. "Mademoiselle, you want rabbit stew? *Oui?"*

"Oh no," I said. "No, not rabbit anything."

"S'il vous plaît." He pointed to the subtitles on my menu—the *English* words just below the French.

"Oh," I said, flushing. I'd been so flustered, I hadn't

even noticed. Then I remembered my manners and replied, *"Merci."*

"I come back," he said.

Mom reached across the table and squeezed my hand. "Relax, sweetie. It's all new, so don't be afraid to ask for help. When you travel, there really are no mistakes—just good learning opportunities."

I exhaled and squeezed her hand back. "Thanks, Mom."

When the waiter returned with a neatly folded white cloth over one arm, I ordered the closest thing I could find to a grilled cheese, the *croque-monsieur.* It was a grilled cheese with ham. It looked a little different from what I usually ordered back home, and I wondered if I'd like the cheese, which had a name I didn't recognize. But I snapped a photo for my blog.

Click!

And I decided I was too hungry not to at least try it.

I took a bite.

One wonderful, amazing bite.

My taste buds filled with butter, ham, and cheese that melted in my mouth. Delicious! I'd have to write about the sandwich on my blog.

I gazed out at the sidewalk and its ever-moving river of tourists and Parisians.

I could try to describe the sandwich, but it would never be the same as tasting it here, on the streets of Paris, seated at an outdoor café with my mom. I guess there are some things you can't learn from a website or a book. Some things, you just have to learn through experience. I gave my mom a thumbs-up and took another big bite.

That afternoon, when we returned our bikes, I spotted the little dog with the "pirate patch" sitting near the *pâtisserie*.

"Mom, that's her! The one I told you about! Hello, little dog," I said softly.

"Oh, I've seen a dog like this before. It's a French bulldog," Mom said.

I giggled. "This one is a *French* French bulldog." I crouched down and held out my hand.

"Careful, Grace," Mom warned. "No matter how

cute she is, we don't know this dog well."

"It's okay," I said. "Sylvie already knows her and she's friendly. Just a little shy at first." The dog wagged her tail, took a few cautious steps, and then stopped several feet away from me. "What's your name? Where's your owner?" I asked soothingly.

She looked back at me with black button eyes.

"Mom, see? She doesn't even have a collar. She's a stray," I said sadly.

"Grace, I'm sure she has a home somewhere."

But I wasn't so sure. The next time I saw this little dog, I'd have something in my pocket to give her, just as Sylvie had done. It was the least I could do.

Lost!
Chapter 6

E ventually, my body started getting used to the time change. Instead of feeling wide-awake in the middle of the night, I started sleeping when it was dark and waking up in the morning.

Unfortunately, though, after a few days of trying new foods, learning new words, and exploring the St. Germain *arrondissement* (or neighborhood), nothing much had changed between me and Sylvie. Instead of feeling like a pair of cousins, we seemed more like a pair of mismatched socks.

One morning I woke up early, only to find Sylvie's bed empty. I wandered sleepily to the kitchen, the apartment unusually quiet.

Mom sat on the couch reading. Napoléon rested above her on the back of the couch, with one paw on Mom's shoulder.

"Mom, where is everybody?" I whispered.

Mom's dimples deepened with her big smile. "Your aunt had a baby last night!"

"Here?"

"No, sweetie. Uncle Bernard took her to the hospital just before midnight."

"Oh! Where's Sylvie?"

"She's there now. Her dad returned an hour ago to take her to the hospital to meet her new little sister."

"A girl?"

Mom nodded.

"What's her name?" I asked, feeling as if I'd missed out on Christmas morning.

"They haven't decided on one yet."

I felt more than a little jealous that I hadn't been woken up, too. I would have loved going with Sylvie to meet her new sister.

The cobwebs finally started to clear from my brain. "Wait," I said to Mom, "I thought the baby wasn't due until the middle of July!"

"She was," said Mom. "But she decided to come early. She arrived at quarter to three this morning."

As I took in this big news, I poured myself a glass

of orange juice and lathered a *croissant* with butter and apricot jam. Before I sat down at the table, I blurted, "Mom, things aren't getting any easier with Sylvie. I feel like she doesn't even want me here."

"Oh, Grace," said Mom, setting down her book. "I'm sorry you feel that way. I think Sylvie is just going through lots of changes right now. That can be hard."

Yeah, well, what about me? I thought grumpily. *I'm in a new country, far away from my friends, and staying with someone who won't even try to speak with me.*

I gazed out the window toward the gray buildings, some with gargoyles, many with bright shutters and flower boxes. I didn't want to be in a bad mood. I was in Paris. And Aunt Sophie had just had a baby. That meant I had a new baby cousin! "I want to meet the baby," I said as brightly as I could.

"Me, too," Mom said with a smile. "I'm sure she'll be beautiful and delightful, and she'll bring lots of joy—along with change—to this little family. We'll go this afternoon, okay?"

I nodded, hoping Mom was right about the "joy" part. Something had to change between me and Sylvie. I crossed my fingers, hoping this baby was it.

Lost!

Her name is Lilou. "Lily" for short. And since she came home from the hospital, I hadn't been able to take my eyes off her.

I'd never seen such tiny fingernails and toenails. When she was sleeping, such sweet expressions came over her rosy lips. She was as perfect as a rosebud!

"I think you and Dad should have another baby," I said to Mom as she held Lily in her arms on the sofa. I snuggled close on one side, breathing in Lily's sweet baby scent.

Mom laughed. "We have you and Josh," she said, "with enough wonderful memories of you two as babies to last us a lifetime."

"Thanks, I guess," I said with a sigh. "Just thought I'd try."

Aunt Sophie was great about letting me hold Lily, too. I had to be seated, and when she handed the baby to me, I made sure to support her head. I was very, very careful. And I was head-over-heels in love with her!

For the first day or two, both Sylvie and I spent hours beside Lily's bassinet, just watching her and talking to her—me in English and Sylvie in French.

But then Lily discovered her lungs, and everything changed. When she cried, everybody in the house heard her. With the windows open much of the time, half the neighborhood probably heard her, too!

I slept with my pillow over my ears.

Sylvie did the same.

Nobody was really getting enough sleep, except for Lily, who had her nights and days confused.

Mom was right. A baby changed lots of things. Aunt Sophie's delivery had required surgery, so she couldn't lift anything for weeks. That meant Mom was on full-time duty—making meals, changing diapers, and bathing Lily—as Aunt Sophie built up her strength. Mom was too tired to stick with her running schedule.

With Mom's help, I changed a few diapers, but I honestly felt more in the way than helpful. And it didn't make things easier for me that Sylvie still disappeared downstairs to the bakery most of each day.

I started to feel really homesick—for Dad, Josh, Grandma, and Grandpa.

I longed to be back in my own home . . . with my

own bed . . . and with my own friends, Ella and Maddy. Part of me wanted to go back to the start of summer and not go to Paris—to stay home instead and start up a business with my friends.

But then I gave myself a talking-to. I didn't want to spend the rest of my visit sulking. If I wasn't happy, it was up to me to change things. I had to come up with an idea—a way to start having more fun. But how? I would just have to keep my eyes open for possibilities.

One evening at dinner, Uncle Bernard apologized for being gone so much. He said this was the busiest season at the *pâtisserie*. "I am happy you are here to help with the baby," he said to Mom.

But then an idea came to me.

"Uncle Bernard," I said. "I love helping at the bakery back home with Grandma and Grandpa. I'd like to help at your bakery—the *pâtisserie*—if you'd let me."

At first he waved away my suggestion, as if it would be too much trouble.

"*Papa*," Sylvie said with a nod of encouragement. "*S'il te plaît?*"

He looked from me to Sylvie and then back again. "*Oui*, Grace. The *pâtisserie* is very busy. You will stay close to my Sylvie and to Colette, our summer intern."

I flashed a grateful smile to Sylvie, and she smiled shyly back. She did want me here after all!

With bright, round eyes under straight-cut bangs, Colette greeted me with a kiss on each cheek. *"Bonjour, Grace!"* She wore a short floral dress and knee-length leggings, but it was her orange-and-purple ruffled apron that I admired the most.

"Bonjour, Colette!"

With the grace and energy of a dancer, she flitted and spun around the bakery, pointing out the bakery oven, the stand mixer, and other appliances in a rush of English and French. I followed very little, but I could tell that Uncle Bernard's bakery employed at least three bakers—one woman and two men. They were all busy rolling, shaping, baking, slicing, and decorating. Each glanced up with a brief nod of hello, but clearly, it was time to work. One of the women grabbed a large tray of strawberry *tartes* and headed for the swinging door, where customers were waiting to purchase the

creations. As the tray passed, I admired how the
berries glistened, each artfully placed on the *tartes*.

In the kitchen of the *pâtisserie*, the smells trans-
ported me back home to First Street Family Bakery. I
felt a sudden pang of homesickness for Grandma and
Grandpa and their bakery, with its heavenly spices and
wrap-you-up warmth from the ovens. Now I understood why Aunt Sophie was drawn to work in a French
bakery. It was similar to Grandma and Grandpa's and
yet quite different, too.

The bakers worked like artists, paying attention
to every detail. At an amazing speed, they cut dough
into triangles and rolled them into *croissants*. Though
Colette was an intern and was still learning, she glided
from task to task with ease. Even Sylvie skillfully
arranged small glazed strawberries points-up on the
tartes.

From the ovens came delicious-smelling treats
that Colette named for me: *pains au chocolat* (chocolate
croissants), *chaussons aux pommes* (apple turnovers), and
pains aux raisins (raisin bread).

At the counters, the bakers worked on chocolate
éclairs, *macarons*, and lemon *meringue* pies. I wished

Grace

Grandma and Grandpa could be here to see all of this!

At first, because Colette asked me to, I just watched everyone else work. I kept scooting out of the way—back toward the walls, back toward the corners. After an hour passed, I began to feel, well, useless. But I knew that wasn't true. I helped out plenty at First Street Family Bakery. I just needed something to do.

Colette turned from whisking eggs at the counter and motioned to me.

At last!

She smiled and made a motion with her hand toward the broom next to the sink. Sweep? I'd rather learn how to bake French treats, but I suppose everyone has to start somewhere. I definitely knew how to operate a broom and dustpan. In dusty patches, flour had spilled across the ceramic tile floor, which I knew from experience could be slippery.

As Colette disappeared into the customer service area, I started to sweep, quiet and curious as a cat. I swept behind the bakers' backs, careful not to disturb their concentration, yet keeping an eye on what everyone was doing. I'd prove I could be trusted with simple tasks, and from there, I'd soon be learning the skills of master French bakers. I swept and swept, building up a good pile of dust, flour, and sugar.

But the very moment I bent down with a dustpan, a breeze blew in. And not through just one door, which might not have been so bad, but through two open doors, creating a cross-current.

Colette returned from the customer area, and at the same time, a delivery person stepped through the back door. A gust of wind whooshed in, picked up my pile, and tossed it like confetti into the air. I watched it swirl, drift, and land—all across baking trays of croissants and bowls filled with cream and meringue.

"Non, non!" Uncle Bernard called out, wagging his finger at me.

My face crumpled. I froze in place. Suddenly, I couldn't even find words in English.

Colette dashed to my side, took the broom and dustpan, swept up quickly, and deposited the floor dustings in the garbage. "Sweep? *Non.*" She pointed to the counter with dirty pots and pans and the nearby sink. "Wash, Grace. Wash."

I'd misunderstood her instructions—I thought she had motioned to the broom. I wanted the earth to open up and swallow me whole.

But that didn't happen.

Everyone stared at me for hours—or what felt like hours—and then looked around at the damage.

"C'est dommage," said Uncle Bernard, shaking his head. Then he set his shoulders and said, *"Recommence!* Begin again."

I felt like such a failure! I'd only wanted to help, but my mistake was costing the bakery time and money by having to start all over.

Glad to turn my back and not have to speak to anyone, I reached for the faucet. I filled the deep stainless steel sinks with hot water and cool rinse water. As I sunk my hands into the hot, soapy water, I squeezed back tears. I scolded myself for not knowing better, for not understanding Colette's sign language, for not understanding French. I washed and scrubbed until my hands turned to wrinkled cranberries. Then I rinsed, dried, and stacked dishes on the nearby counter.

When I turned around, everyone was busy again.

I walked quietly toward Colette. "May I go outside for a few minutes?" I asked.

As her eyes met mine, I blinked back tears.

⌒ *Lost!* ⌒

Colette gave me an understanding smile and patted my shoulder. *"Oui."* Then she made a closing motion with her thumb and forefinger. "Short time?" she asked.

I nodded.

I hurried out the back door, which opened onto a narrow cobblestone street. Across the street, neon green letters formed a word I understood: *PHARMA-CIE.* I was pretty sure they sold everything you could need for a sore throat, a runny nose, or an upset stomach. I wondered what they would say if I went in and asked, "Do you have something for when you feel like a failure?"

But then, I didn't know enough French to ask the question.

Or to make a joke.

I leaned against the stone wall of the building. I had wanted to cry, but the moment had passed. Instead, I drew in deep, full breaths as a throng of tourists biked by, laughing and speaking a language I didn't understand. I knew I was supposed to be having a great time here in Paris, but . . .

Across the street, a gray cat sunned itself on a window ledge, beside a leafy tree. It stretched, arched its back, and then crawled out onto the branch. It dropped to the sidewalk and sauntered off to my left, flicking the tip of its crooked tail.

I drew another breath. *So you made a mistake,* I told myself. *At least you won't make that one again.* At a bakery, sweeping is for the end of the day, not for in the middle of things.

Suddenly, from my right, approached the little black-and-white dog. Head high, she trotted right toward me.

"Bonjour, petite chienne," I called softly.

I held my breath, hoping she wouldn't dart off. I needed her company today more than ever. "Know what? I just destroyed a morning's worth of work in there," I confided in her.

She sat a few feet away and cocked her head, looking through her pirate's patch with those big eyes.

But then a flash of gray fur caught her attention, and she darted across the street. I breathed a sigh of relief that no cars had been coming.

"*Petite chienne!* Come back!" I called.

But she was clearly after the cat, who darted around the corner building.

I decided to follow, just for a while. The little dog was probably hungry, and I could help fix that.

I looked both ways, crossed toward the pharmacy, and then hurried on around the corner. The cat wasn't very far ahead of the dog, and I wondered if this was a game they'd played before. The street opened up beyond shops and outdoor cafés onto a familiar square—the one near towering St. Sulpice church.

I'd seen the square from the taxi on my first day here. In the center of the square, water flowed down the sides of a fountain, past the fierce faces of lions carved into the stone. Above them sat the sculptures of four solemn bishops, gazing east, west, north, and south.

I knew exactly where I was right now, and I promised myself I'd head straight back. If I could just get the little dog to trust me and lure her back to the bakery . . .

The cat darted up into the branches of a tree. The dog yipped for a few moments and then turned to lap water that overflowed from the fountain onto the cobblestones.

"Here, pup," I said, walking slowly closer and closer.

But the moment I reached for her, she darted from my grasp. Then she stopped a few yards off and wagged her tail, as if challenging me to a new game. I chased her. We went around and around the fountain, and I finally stopped to catch my breath in the shade.

"Me-owwww." The cat inched its way down the tree trunk and then leaped to the ground. It bolted, and the little dog ran after it.

I realized this game could go on forever. And I remembered my promise to Colette: just a short time outside. Uh-oh. I'd been away a little longer than I'd planned. I'd better hurry back!

I started off toward one of the streets. But which *rue* was it? I turned in a full circle, studying the square. The narrow streets, surrounding shops, and restaurants all looked familiar. I couldn't get my bearings. I felt turned around, thrown off. I wasn't sure where to head, which street to take back.

Was I lost? I hated to admit it. And I didn't want to cause any more trouble for anyone today. My throat tightened and my head buzzed.

Start walking, I told myself, *and see where a street takes you.*

No! I could almost hear Dad's words in my head: *Stay put. Wait for someone to find you.*

On one street, a man in a bright green uniform pushed a broom. On the sidewalk of another, an elderly woman walked a tiny white dog.

I decided on the woman. I ran to her, slowing down so as not to frighten her. *"Madame, parlez-vous anglais?"*

She glanced at me and shook her head, but then pointed to a shop window with children's clothing. Maybe somebody there . . .

I stepped in the doorway. Clothes were displayed around the shop as if each item was a piece of art. A woman greeted me from behind a small counter. *"Bonjour, Mademoiselle!"*

"Bonjour, Madame! Do you know where the bakery is?"

"Ah, oui." She pointed down the street.

I smiled. *"Merci!"*

But when I arrived at the storefront, it wasn't Uncle Bernard's *pâtisserie.* The sign said *Boulangerie,* and the display window was filled with *baguettes* and buns. My heart sank. I had forgotten that there were two types of bakeries in Paris—*pâtisseries* that made pastries, and *boulangeries* that made mostly breads.

I turned around and walked purposely back toward the square and the fierce lions. I circled the fountain under the stern glare of the stone men seated at its top.

I stopped in one place.

If I hadn't rushed out of the *pâtisserie* without my backpack, I'd have had a travel book or a map on me now. And maybe, maybe I could have figured out the way back from here. But I was empty-handed.

At home I knew every street and shortcut, every shop on First Street and many of the owners, too.

But here . . . No matter how I slowly spun around, hoping to see a familiar landmark, no matter how many times I walked around the fountain, I kept coming back to one dizzying conclusion.

I was *lost*.

A New Friend

Chapter 7

$\mathcal{T}$he sight of two bicyclists coming toward me had never looked better. Colette and Sylvie biked side by side, taking turns calling out my name. "Grace!"

"Hello! Over here!" Tears of relief fell down my cheeks.

The girls circled to the other side of the fountain, and for a second, panic welled up in me. What if they didn't hear me? What if they'd turned down one of the streets away from me?

But in seconds, they appeared around the edge of the fountain and spotted me. Relief spread across their faces as they rolled to a stop. I expected a scolding from Colette and could barely look her in the eye.

"I'm sorry," I said—and broke promptly into sobs. "I followed the little dog here—*petite chienne*—and would have come right back, but I . . . I . . . " Tears streamed down my face.

Colette jumped off her bike. "Poor Grace," she said, handing me a tissue from her shoulder bag.

I blew my nose.

Sylvie hugged me, as if she understood how terrible it had felt to be lost—and how relieved I felt to be found.

And then they walked their bikes alongside me down the right street toward home.

Returning to the bakery with their help was easy. Of course I should have noticed the bronze drinking fountain with the sculpted women, and the orange awning of another café. But even those landmarks began to blur through my tears.

Back at the apartment, Mom gave me a one-on-one talk all about how I couldn't get lost again. I was in another country, she reminded me. And I owed an apology to my aunt and uncle for the unnecessary worry I'd put them through, not to mention her own worries.

"I'm sorry," I told Mom.

ᒪᑫ A New Friend ᑫᒪ

"Je regrette," I said to Uncle Bernard and Aunt Sophie.

All of my apologies were met with hugs. Even Sylvie was acting extra nice.

After dinner, I went to bed early, utterly exhausted. Sylvie surprised me by bringing in a tray with two cups of tea and two chocolate *truffles*. She offered me a cup. "Grace, you like?"

I nodded, and then sat up cross-legged and took the cup from the tray.

She set the tray on her bedside table and turned to her bed with her cup of tea. But then she glanced back at me and pointed to the end of my mattress. *"S'il te plaît?"* she asked. "Please? I sit?"

"Oui!" I said. And there, for a few sweet minutes, we had our own private tea party. We didn't talk a lot, but for the first time, I felt as if I was finally having fun with my cousin—as if we were actually becoming friends.

The next morning during Mom's coffee time, I sat

with her on the couch with my tablet and logged on to e-mail.

Sylvie had already headed downstairs to help out in the *pâtisserie*. But I wasn't quite ready to show my face there yet—if ever again. I needed to hear from my friends back home, and I was thrilled to see an e-mail waiting for me from Maddy:

> *Hi Grace! Good news here. We've started a business! It's called "Maddy and Ella's Dog-Walking Service." Our slogan is "We walk your dog so that you don't have to!!!"*

What? My friends were supposed to wait for me!

I couldn't even read the rest of the message. I stared at the ceiling.

Great.

Just great.

I huffed.

"What's bothering you?" Mom asked, looking over my shoulder.

"Maddy and Ella started their own dog-walking business—without me. They said they were going to wait until I returned."

⌒ A New Friend ⌒

Mom brushed my hair back over my shoulder. "That hurts, huh?" she said gently.

"Uh, yeah."

I turned back to the rest of Maddy's e-mail. My friends already had five customers signed up for dog-walking. Maddy had printed out flyers to hand out to family and friends.

I typed a quick reply:

I thought we were going to do a business together.

The answer came later that morning, short and swift as a slap in the face:

When you get back, we can add your name.

I instantly hit the "log out" button.

I felt terrible. Clearly my friends were going on with their lives and doing fine without me.

I felt so left out!

And I wasn't doing just fine without them. I thought of the scene I'd made at the *pâtisserie* with the broom, and then of getting lost and needing Colette and Sylvie to come find me. At home, I was used to doing things pretty well, especially baking. Here I felt like a klutz and a fool! I wanted to go home. Now.

But I still had several weeks to go here. After that, would Ella and Maddy still want to add me to their business? Would they even remember how to spell my name?

Sylvie went downstairs to help in the *pâtisserie* that afternoon, but I did my best to avoid it. Instead, I helped change a few diapers. I helped with dishes. I even asked to rock Lily when she was fussy. "Mom, let me try," I said. I sat back on the rocking chair, and Mom placed Lily gently in my arms.

But the moment she did, beautiful, sweet Lily turned into red-faced, wailing Lily!

She fussed and cried, and nothing I did or said helped. I talked soothingly. I sang to her. I offered her a bottle. But I didn't have the magic touch and quickly handed her back to Mom. I couldn't even help with a baby!

ᴄ~ A New Friend ~ᴐ

That night, I couldn't wait to video-chat with Dad. He'd help me. He always seems to know what to ask or say to help me get unstuck.

When his face appeared on the screen, with the living room bookcase in the background, I felt relieved. "Hi, Dad!" I hadn't even realized how much I'd been missing him.

"Hi, Grace," he said with a big smile. "Great to see you and hear your voice, sweetie. How are you?"

I nearly cried when he asked that. But I held it together long enough to get my story out. "I made a mess at the bakery yesterday," I explained, "and cost Uncle Bernard a lot of work. And then I got lost and made everyone worry. And then . . . my friends . . . started a business without me." I suddenly started to cry—I couldn't help it!

"Oh, now, Grace," Dad said. "It's okay. I'm right here. You talk when you can."

I took a few deep breaths and tried to pull myself together. "I miss you, Dad. And Josh. And I have three more weeks here. And Sylvie is starting to act nice to me, but she's at the bakery all day . . . and . . . and . . ."

"I hear you're going through a rough patch, Grace,"

Dad said in his calm, reassuring way. "I'd give you a
hug if I were there. But I'm not. So I'm going to pose
a question instead for you to think about. You're not
happy, but you have several more weeks there. And so
here's the question: What are you going to do about it?"

"Um . . ."

"No need to answer. Just think about it. You're full
of ideas, Grace. You'll find the answer you need."

I wished I felt as sure about that as Dad did.
"Thanks," I said to him, "but I don't know."

"You will, sweetie. I know you will," he said again.
"Now, can I say hi to your mom real quick?"

I nodded, but I didn't call my mom over quite yet. "I
love you, Dad," I said, wishing I could give him a hug.

"I love you, too, Grace," he said in his warm voice.

Later, as I tried to go to sleep, Dad's words played
over and over through my head. *So? What are you going
to do about it?*

I didn't know.

Sometime during the night, I woke to Napoléon
padding slowly around me, as if he knew I needed a
friend. He settled softly behind the crook of my legs,
and warmed by his company, I fell back to sleep.

⌒ A New Friend ⌒

In the morning, he was gone.

The next afternoon, after helping Mom make a spinach *quiche* for dinner, I gazed out the apartment window. Below, a guitarist strummed on the street corner with a young woman beside him, swaying as she sang. Though I didn't understand the French lyrics, their melodies drifted up to me, soft and touching. I sighed.

I had a few weeks left in Paris, and I needed to try to make the most of it.

When I saw the little black-and-white dog amble down the sidewalk, I sat up straight and said, "Mom, I want to sit outside for a bit."

"Do I need to remind you to stay close?" she said with one of those looks.

I shook my head. "I know."

I grabbed a slice of *baguette* and a lonely chunk of cheese from the fridge and headed down the stairs.

I sat quietly at one of the round tables outside the *pâtisserie*. I wouldn't chase the dog. I wouldn't try to catch her. I would just be there for her if she wanted to say hi. I didn't even look for her. Instead, I soaked in the music as the man with the ponytail strummed, sometimes joining in song with the woman. They met each other's eyes often with a smile.

There it was right in front of me. The City of Love.

And just then, someone nudged my leg. I glanced down into big, round black eyes. "Oh, it's you," I said casually, even though my heart was leaping. "Well, I'm just sitting here. You can hang out with me if you like." I ate a little bread and cheese, and then looked at the little dog.

She whined.

"Oh? You want some?"

She made a sound somewhere between a moan and a growl.

"Are you talking to me?"

Her tail wagged.

I offered her a few treats, which she took gently from my hand. Then I glanced back at the musicians.

The little dog talked again, a moaning whine this time. Sitting back on her haunches, she pushed her wet nose under my hand.

"What? You want me to pet you?" I gave her

another piece of bread and cheese. It disappeared instantly. I dangled my hand at my side. Again, she brushed under it. That's when I started to pet her shoulders.

She groaned.

I scratched her neck and under her chin.

She moaned.

With all the scratching and petting, I'd managed to stir up a stinky smell. "You're cute, but you really need a bath," I said. "If you were my dog, I'd give you one right now with lots of shampoo!"

She wagged her tail and licked my hand as if to say she wouldn't mind.

I sighed. "I wish I could take you in and give you a home. But I don't live here. Still, even a stray should have a name. Let's see . . . You're little, like *macarons*. A little rough on the outside, but on the inside?"

She cocked her head, as if listening intently to my every word.

I laughed. "On the inside, you're all sweetness, like those chocolate-covered round candies—*bonbons au chocolat*. I know! I'm going to call you 'Bonbon.'"

She wagged her tail again, and that was how

I knew the name would stick.

I couldn't believe I was actually petting my new little friend. I'd waited for this for so long, and finally, my patience and persistence had paid off! I wished some of my good luck with Bonbon would rub off on everything else: that Sylvie and I would grow closer, that my friends back home wouldn't forget about me, and that I could somehow find the courage to go back into the kitchen of the *pâtisserie*.

I suddenly heard Dad's voice in my mind. *What are you going to do about it?*

I looked down into Bonbon's sweet face, and then I knew just what I would do.

I would try again.

I would keep trying with Sylvie and in the *pâtisserie*, just as I had with Bonbon.

I wouldn't give up.

Before dinner, I put out a bowl of water for Bonbon. Uncle Bernard said he didn't think it was a good idea, but he didn't forbid me.

A New Friend

"We should call authorities, yes?" he said across the dinner table to Aunt Sophie.

She held Lily in her arms and shook her head uncertainly. "I'm afraid the dog will be put to sleep," she said. "Let's hope someone takes her in."

Sylvie must have been following some of the conversation. She looked at her father with those big brown eyes of hers. *"Papa? S'il te plaît?"*

"Non, Sylvie." He pointed toward Lily and then to Napoléon stretched out across the back of the sofa. I didn't understand all he said in French to Sylvie, but I could tell from the drop in her shoulders that adding a dog to their family was out of the question.

Sylvie looked at me sadly, but I did my best to force a smile onto my face. I didn't know how to help Bonbon, but I was determined to keep trying.

Bastille Day
Chapter 8

*T*he next day, I did two things. First, I asked Mom if I could use my travel allowance to buy dog food for Bonbon at the pet supply store a few blocks away. I couldn't give her a home, but I could give her food and water—and plenty of love.

The second thing I did was march back downstairs to help out at the *pâtisserie* with Mom's words sounding in my head: *When you travel, there really are no mistakes— just learning opportunities.* I wasn't going to learn anything if I couldn't allow myself to make a few mistakes along the way. So I decided that if I wanted to have more fun during the rest of my stay, I had to try again.

That first morning back in the *pâtisserie,* I proved I was a very skilled dishwasher.

I was a skilled floor sweeper, too, now that I knew to sweep the floor only when counters were clear of food. Some mistakes you make only once.

Now that I had jumped in, Colette found more and more things for me to do. "Grace, can you do?" She demonstrated cracking one egg into a bowl with one hand.

I shook my head.

So she taught me how to crack an egg with one hand, without breaking the yolk. It took a little practice, but before long . . . *voilà*! She taught me how to properly use a whisk to make whipped cream. And she taught me how to carefully use a piping bag to fill *éclairs*.

I learned to stay clear of the pathway between the ovens and the counters when trays of anything hot were coming out. But oh, the air was warm and sweet with yeasty baked goods and melted sugar and butter!

The next morning when I woke up, Sylvie was gone. Was she already downstairs? I quickly got dressed, wondering what new techniques Colette might teach me today in the *pâtisserie*. As I dashed out of the bedroom, Mom called to me from the kitchen.

"Happy Bastille Day, Grace!" she said in a singsong voice.

"Happy what?" I asked, stepping into the kitchen.

"*Bastille* Day," Mom repeated. "France's day of independence. July fourteenth here is a lot like July fourth back home. Come sit and I'll tell you about it."

I was torn—eager to get downstairs. But Mom had that look on her face that said breakfast was more of an order than a request. So I trooped to the table, where she had a *croissant* waiting for me.

"France had a revolution much like ours," Mom explained, passing me the jam. "We threw off being governed by England, an ocean away. Here, the people were overtaxed and hungry, and they didn't want to be governed by their kings and queens any longer. On July 14, 1789, they stormed the Bastille, a fortress and prison in Paris, which began the revolution."

Mom was such a teacher! But I couldn't resist asking, "And then what happened?"

"Well, King Louis the Sixteenth was taken to the *guillotine* and beheaded."

I sucked in my breath. "And the queen?"

"The queen at the time was Marie Antoinette. They

arrested her, too, and held her in a tower here on the Seine. Eventually, she lost her head, too."

"Ouch," I said, a bite of *croissant* sticking in my throat.

"*Revolution* comes from the word *revolt*," Mom continued. "When people feel voiceless, they sometimes revolt and take matters into their own hands. And today the people of France are celebrating that revolution—or the new government that was formed because of it. There'll be parades and maybe fireworks later. Sound like fun?"

I nodded. But the word *fun* made me think of the *pâtisserie*. I swallowed my last bite and chugged my juice. "Can I be done?" I asked Mom.

She grinned and nodded. "Yes, Grace," she said. "Your history lesson is done. Get on downstairs."

I gave Mom a quick hug and raced down the narrow stairs and into the *pâtisserie* kitchen, where I found Uncle Bernard, Sylvie, and Colette hard at work.

"Happy Bastille Day!" I announced.

Sylvie looked up in surprise. "Bastille Day? Ah, *la prise de la Bastille!* Happy Bastille Day, Grace," she said, smiling.

Grace

Uncle Bernard nodded. "Yes, a day to celebrate. You've all been working very hard. This afternoon you go to *Berthillon* shop. Very famous!" Then he added in French, *"Allez donc vous prendre une glace."*

A smile stretched across Sylvie's face, and I waited in suspense to hear what had been said.

Colette translated for me. *"De la glace,* Grace. Ice cream."

I gave a thumbs-up. Ice cream—everywhere—is a treat!

When afternoon came, I was more than ready for our bike ride to Berthillon. I was thrilled to go on an outing with Colette. Sylvie was still pretty quiet around me, but we managed to exchange a few words here and there. With Colette I felt a little freer. She could, after all, speak my language.

Colette tucked her black ruffled skirt beneath her as she jumped onto her bike. I wasn't surprised anymore to see women in dresses and men in business suits on bikes, zipping around Paris.

Bastille Day

I was riding Aunt Sophie's bike today, with the seat lowered just enough to fit me. As I trailed Colette and Sylvie down the cobblestone street, I noticed that many of the shops had signs in the window that read *fermé,* which must mean "closed." And some of the shops had flags and banners stretched over their awnings in honor of Bastille Day.

The French flag is blue, white, and red—the same colors as our flag! I noticed that people were wearing patriotic-colored clothing, too. As one teenage boy flew by us on his bike, I saw a bold French flag painted on his cheek. Sylvie caught it, too, and we exchanged smiles.

"Girls," Colette called over her shoulder, "first we go to *les Halles.*"

We crossed the river, and Sylvie and I followed Colette like little ducklings. I wasn't about to get lost again.

"*Le Louvre,*" Colette said, biking into an expansive stone square between brick buildings. At the center of the square stood a glass pyramid. It was such a modern design in the middle of this old city. Colette explained in words and gestures that it was the entrance to the vast surrounding museum, where lines of visitors seemed to extend for miles. I was glad to be biking, instead of standing in line.

Les Halles turned out to be a nearby neighborhood famous for its baking and cooking shops. I'd landed in a dreamworld!

We parked our bikes, and then Colette pulled out a piece of paper with a short list of items.

"Girls," she said to me and Sylvie, holding up the list for us to read. "We need for *La Pâtisserie*." She repeated in French for Sylvie.

The list of items was all in French. *"En anglais, s'il te plaît?"* I asked, pointing to the words. "In English, please?"

Colette quickly interpreted, and then we were off looking for pastry rings, pastry brushes, and more, as if on a scavenger hunt together.

My head spun as I followed Colette and Sylvie in and out of shops filled with every sort of baking pan and cookware imaginable. I saw rows of cooking utensils. Stoneware dishes of yellow, red, white, black, and eggplant purple. Special pans and dishes for making many of the French treats I'd come to love, such as madeleines, *tartes,* and *crème brûlée*—that yummy custard with a caramelized top.

At one shop, when Colette asked for baking paper, a man in a tie climbed to the top of a ladder to retrieve the paper from a tall stack of supplies.

At another shop, Sylvie paused to hold up a fake red lobster and struck a pose. It was half her size! I laughed and whipped out my phone.

Click!

It took some effort, but eventually we helped Colette find everything on her list.

"*Voilà!*" I said, hopping on my bike after Colette.

"Mission accomplished!" Sylvie chimed in from behind me, her English taking me by surprise.

I started to giggle. "*Mission accomplished?* Where did you learn that?" I called over my shoulder.

But she just laughed and then, like a parrot, repeated it again. "Mission accomplished!" Hearing such a familiar phrase spoken in Sylvie's French accent cracked me up. Who knew running errands could be so much fun?

We biked back across another bridge onto a little island called *Île Saint-Louis*. On the corner of an outdoor café, I spotted a sign with a long list of ice cream flavors.

"Berthillon!" Sylvie called with a big smile.

I quickly realized that the worst part about visiting Berthillon, the famous place to stop for ice cream, was making a decision. I finally settled on *noisette* and *framboise*—hazelnut and raspberry. Instead of one scoop on top of the other, the little cake cone held two scoops side by side. Cute!

We leaned over the stone wall with our cones, licking them faster than the sun could melt them away. Below, long tourist boats drifted by, with guides on board giving the history of the little island and the Notre Dame cathedral up ahead.

I waved and a few boaters waved back.

I thought back to my first few days here and my visit to the famous cathedral with Mom. I'd been pretty tense at first, trying to figure out this new world around me. Everything had felt so strange, so different then. But in only a few weeks' time, some things were starting to seem familiar. I was feeling more at home, and I couldn't believe that today, I was actually out exploring the heart of Paris with Colette and Sylvie. I smiled at them as they licked their cones.

Colette asked, *"Aimes-tu la glace,* Grace?"

Sylvie repeated the question in English. "Do you like ice cream, Grace?"

"Like it?" I took another lick, as if I wasn't quite sure. I let my tongue savor the flavors. "No, I don't like it."

For a moment, they both looked disappointed, but I didn't let them worry for long.

"I don't *like* it," I said again. *"Je t'aime!"*

Sylvie giggled and corrected me. *"Je l'aime."*

"Oui!" I said, taking another lick. "I love it!"

Sylvie giggled again, which made the ice cream taste that much sweeter.

As we biked back across the bridge toward the *pâtisserie,* we came upon two musicians—an accordion player and a violinist—with an open case at their feet filled with coins. They were playing an energetic marching song, like something you might hear at the start of a sports event, and the man playing the accordion was singing in a deep, proud voice.

Colette put up her hand, signaling to us that she wanted to stop. We joined her and pulled off to the side near the musicians, where a few other people were gathering, too, and singing along.

"*La Marseillaise*," she whispered to me. "Our . . . how do you say . . . national song."

I let the music flow through me as Colette translated the lyrics. As the accordion player sang "*Marchons! Marchons!*" Colette leaned toward me and whispered, "March! March!" And I wanted to! Or at least to sing along with the others, whose voices swelled together into one wonderful chorus.

As the song came to an end, we applauded and turned back toward our bikes. But then the musicians began something new: a sweet melody that caught Colette's attention. Her eyes lit up and she swayed slightly, moving with the rhythm. And then she began to sing. Her voice fluttered up and around us, as unexpectedly beautiful as a pigeon in flight.

I turned to Sylvie, who looked equally surprised.

Bastille Day

The accordion player smiled through his short gray beard. The violinist, a woman with volumes of red hair, nodded approvingly at Colette.

Colette sang on, seeming completely confident and at ease. *I could never do that!* I thought to myself, wishing I had the courage to just jump in and do something unexpected. But then I remembered that I'd already done many things in Paris that I hadn't thought I could do. Here, everything seemed . . . I struggled for the right word. I don't know. *Lighter,* as if the very air was filled with something magical—filled with possibility.

I wished that I had researched some French songs—practiced them—so that I would be ready for this moment. But as much as I like to plan ahead, I guess there are some moments you just can't plan for. *Stay loose,* Mom had said to me at the start of our trip. Maybe it was time for me to let go a little, to loosen up and take some risks.

When the musicians started in with *"Frère Jacques,"* a song I knew, I felt as if they were playing it just for me. Before I could change my mind, I tossed caution to the wind, stepped into the circle, and joined in singing. Suddenly Sylvie was beside me, and together we were singing our hearts out. A small crowd gathered again, and people started tossing more coins into the open violin case.

I smiled ear to ear as I sang, sharing this moment of fame with Sylvie and Colette. When the song ended and some of the people around us clapped, Sylvie and I burst into laughter. I felt so good—so free!

When the musicians offered to share some of their tips with us, Colette shook her head and just said, *"Merci."* The musicians bowed in our direction and then waved good-bye as we got back on our bikes.

"Au revoir!" we called as we began to pedal away. And long after we reached the other side of the bridge, I could still hear the beautiful sound of that violin.

We took a different route home, because several streets were closed for a parade. I could hear the marching band in the distance, and when a few military planes flew overhead, I ducked my head—which made Sylvie laugh behind me.

When we reached *La Pâtisserie*, the little stray dog

was already hanging out by the front door, ready for an early dinner. I quickly ducked inside to get the bag of dog food and refilled her empty bowl.

Just then, we heard the explosion of fireworks from somewhere nearby. Bonbon crouched down low, ready to run. "It's okay, puppy," I said in a soothing voice. "It's just fireworks. Happy Bastille Day, Bonbon."

"Bonbon?" Sylvie asked with a tilt of her head.

"She needed a name," I explained. I wondered if it bothered Sylvie that I'd gone ahead and named the little dog.

"*Tu t'appelles* Bonbon," she said and ran her hand lightly over the dog's upright ears. She flashed me a smile, and I smiled back.

"She needs a home," Colette said, standing nearby. "You take her to U.S., Grace?"

I shook my head. "No. That's a long way from here, and my mom says no. Can you take her home, Colette?"

"*Je regrette.* I'm sorry. My *maman*, my mother, how you say?" She faked a sneeze.

"Allergies?" I asked.

"*Oui.*"

Sylvie sighed, as if she knew precisely what I was feeling. Unfortunately, neither of us could come to Bonbon's rescue.

Baking with Colette

Chapter 9

*D*espite a rain pattering against our bedroom window, I woke up the next morning humming *"Frère Jacques."* Remembering our moment with the street musicians, I felt a new surge of confidence. I'd dived straight into the music with Colette and Sylvie. I hadn't planned for it—I had just done it! I'd made some mistakes, but I'd also had lots of fun.

Sylvie and I had enjoyed Bastille Day, a day to celebrate French independence. I smiled to myself, realizing that *I* felt a new sense of independence, too. Now that I was learning to jump into new situations, I wanted to experience everything here while I could. I couldn't get enough!

I would have loved to say all this to Sylvie, but it was too much for her to understand—or for me to say in French. Instead, I said, *"Bonjour*, Sylvie!"

"*Bonjour*, Grace!" she replied. "*Comment vas-tu?*"

This time I had the answer to "How are you?" I replied, "*Je vais bien.*"

And I meant it.

I was fine. *More* than fine.

Poor Lily. She, unfortunately, was not doing as well as I was today. She had a cold. Her cute little nose was red, chafed, and running.

Apparently Aunt Sophie had been up all night with her. While she slept in with her door half closed, Mom tried giving Lily a bottle. But Lily was so stuffed up and her nose so gunky that she had trouble breathing and taking the bottle at the same time. In frustration, Lily squeezed her eyes tight and cried harder.

"Is she going to be okay?" I asked as Mom walked the baby up and down the hallway, around the kitchen and living area, and then down the hallway again.

"Yes, she'll be fine," Mom said. "Still, I'd forgotten how hard it is when a baby gets sick."

"Did I get sick—I mean, when I was a baby?"

I asked. "Did you walk me like that?"

"Well, you were a pretty healthy baby. But what I learned early on was that you didn't want to be walked like this. Josh did. But you wanted to be put down in your crib. I think you wanted to figure things out on your own."

Mom turned and made the circuit again, and as she came back my way, Lily stopped crying. Then Mom sat down in the rocker near a table full of baby supplies. She used a small rubber bulb to gently suction Lily's runny nose.

I scrunched up my face. "Don't try that thing on me."

Mom shrugged. "Well, she's too young to blow her nose into a tissue. We have to help her somehow."

But the device helped. Somebody somewhere must have had a baby who needed help, and that somebody came up with a creative solution. *Another good idea*, I thought to myself.

Soon Lily started breathing a little more freely, and Mom offered her a bottle again. "There you go, little girl."

Mom laughed softly. "Honey, I remember the day

you found your thumb," she said, glancing up at me. "It was as if you'd been searching for the answer, and I could almost see a little lightbulb go on in your eyes. At that moment, apparently your thumb was it."

I smiled. "Good thing I don't need my thumb anymore."

"No, now you're good," Mom said. "You're fine as long as you can jump on a computer to research whatever springs to that busy mind of yours, or head to a kitchen to do some baking."

"True," I replied.

I watched Mom finish giving little Lily her bottle. They looked so sweet together. This moment deserved a photo.

Click!

Then I asked Mom if I could e-mail the photo to Grandma and Grandpa.

I was surprised when Grandma e-mailed me right back to thank me. She must have finally figured out her new laptop.

Grandma: *What a little sweetheart! I wish we could be there to see our new grandbaby in person, but the bakery is* *too busy for us to leave in the summer. It makes me happy, though, that you and your mom are there to help out.*

Me: *Speaking of helping out, Grandma, I keep wishing I could do more actual baking here. You know, real French stuff.*

Grandma: *Maybe you just need to ask?*

I smiled. Sometimes the simplest answers were the hardest ones to see.

Me: *Yeah. Maybe I just need to ask. Thanks, Grandma!*

Downstairs at the *pâtisserie,* soft French music came from Colette's phone. I hadn't heard music in the *pâtisserie* kitchen before. Maybe she was trying something new, too.

"I like it," I whispered.

"Good!" she whispered back. "But others?"

Nobody in the kitchen complained about the music, and as her phone app shuffled through various songs and artists, Colette sometimes sang along. Her voice was like wind chimes added to the pleasant whir of chatter, mixing machines, chopping, and oven timers.

After I finished a first round of dishwashing, I was ready to take on more responsibilities. But I needed to master a few basic words first.

I stood at Sylvie's elbow as she cut a *génoise* cake with a pastry knife.

"Sylvie?"

She turned.

I pointed to a bowl on the counter. I now knew how to ask "What is this?"

"Qu'est-ce que c'est?"

"Un cul de poule," she replied.

I repeated the words slowly. Then I pointed to a wooden mixing spoon. *"Qu'est-ce que c'est?"*

"Une spatule en bois," she said.

Sylvie beamed, seeming eager to help. As we stepped around the bakery, I pointed and asked more questions. She helped me learn the French words for *apron, oven, door,* and *floor.* I learned how to say *spoon, measuring cup, plate, small bowls, medium bowls,* and *large bowls* in French. She taught me words for *baking, stir-*

ring, whisking, beating, frosting, decorating, and *sprinkling.*
I wouldn't remember all the words after hearing them
only once, but I started to recognize some of them right
away from the bakers as they worked and talked with
one another.

I was only beginning. I had so much to learn. But
now I felt hungry, ready to sponge up every little word
and phrase and skill around me.

Then Sylvie started testing me. *"Qu'est-ce que c'est?"*
She was the teacher.

I tried to be a smart student, but when I confused
words or butchered saying a word, Sylvie cracked up.

"Hey! You wouldn't be a good teacher if you
laughed whenever your students made mistakes,"
I said, smiling.

She was still giggling, even though I knew she
didn't get what I'd said. But Colette laughed out loud.

Then I started to giggle, too. I couldn't help it! I tried
to swallow my next outburst, but I couldn't. Pretty soon
we were all giggling so loud that Uncle Bernard looked
over our way.

And we giggled two seconds longer.

I drew a deep breath and made myself stop.

$\mathcal{C}$ Grace $\mathcal{O}$

"Colette," I finally ventured. "At home, I love to bake. Can you teach me how to bake here?"

"Oui, oui!" She looked over at Sylvie, who was brushing egg white on something. "Sylvie," she began, and then rattled off a whole lot of French I couldn't understand.

Sylvie finished the last of what she was doing and then joined us for what I silently called "Baking with Colette" class.

Over the next few days, Colette took us through several recipes. First were the *madeleines*. We mixed flour, salt, sugar, and baking powder, and then added egg yolk, melted butter, and slightly beaten egg whites.

The recipe should have been easy, I thought, but I made a few blunders.

With all of the measurements in metric, it felt weird measuring to the nearest gram or milliliter. Where were my familiar cups and tablespoons? I ruined a whole bowl of batter by measuring out 25 grams of salt instead of 2.5 grams—or a half teaspoon.

When Colette sampled the batter, she made a face. "Start again," she said and quickly emptied the bowl's contents into the garbage.

I was so embarrassed. Back home, I would have known the difference between ten teaspoons of salt and a half teaspoon. But here, I was so focused on grams that I started thinking I was measuring sugar instead of salt.

Yuck!

After that mistake, I gave myself my own time-out—or at least time to better understand these new measurements. And after that, I made myself return to my dictionary and refresh my memory of important baking words:

sel (salt)
sucre (sugar)
farine (flour)

By the end of one workday, we were putting the finishing touches on a vanilla *millefeuille,* a layered pastry with a glazed top. The swirled chocolate and vanilla icing was so beautiful, almost like a painting. I thought of the lines waiting to get into the art museum, the Louvre. Wasn't baking an art, too?

"C'est beau!" said Sylvie, admiring our creation.

"We should taste, *oui*?" Colette said.

We cleaned up, hung up our aprons, and arranged slices of the *millefeuille* on pretty plates. Then we sat outside the *pâtisserie*. The shade of stone buildings fell across our little table and the beautiful French treat that I'd actually helped bake. I felt so proud, and amazed that despite my mistakes, I'd learned some really cool new baking skills. I pulled out my phone.

Click!

"Do you want to look or eat?" Colette asked me and Sylvie.

I turned to Sylvie. I couldn't tell if she understood or not. What was the phrase? Then it came to me. "Sylvie. *Veux-tu manger?*"

"*Oui, oui!*" She laughed and then took a bite.

"*Bon appétit!*" Colette said.

I joined in, chewing slowly and letting the flavors linger on my taste buds.

Colette and Sylvie both waited for my opinion.

"Ooo-la-la!" I said.

That evening, I posted our bakery creation on my blog. My caption: *Art You Can Eat!*

Under a late-afternoon sun, I biked after Mom as
she jogged. But every few blocks I had to stop to take
pictures. I couldn't help it! I snapped photos of the
display cases in every *boulangerie* and *pâtisserie* we
passed.

Click-click-click-click-click!

"Grace," Mom scolded as I caught up to her. I
straddled my bike beside her, waiting for her to catch
her breath before the light turned green.

Mom leaned forward with her hands on her thighs,
talking in short spurts. "Between Lily's cold . . ." she
said, "and now your obsession with taking photos . . .
on every block . . . I wonder if I'll ever . . . get back to
my running routine."

She took a few long, deep breaths and then began
talking again, more to the pavement than to me. "I
thought . . . I could manage to stay on track . . . while
we're here . . . but I've fallen . . . way behind schedule."

I wasn't sure what to say at first. Mom sounded so
down. But then I thought of what she might say to me
if I were feeling that way. "Mom," I said. "You're in

Paris. Did you think everything would be the same as at home?"

She hesitated and then said, "Of course not."

"So don't be so hard on yourself. Try to stay loose," I added. I stepped in front of her and shook out my arms and legs as dramatically as I could, just as she'd done when we'd first arrived at the airport here.

Mom stared at me with a straight face for a second or two, as if deciding whether to laugh out loud or scold me again, but then she broke into a smile. "Look who's the teacher now."

When the light turned green, she was ready to run again. We crossed toward the river, where a painter was at his easel capturing Notre Dame towering above the shimmering Seine. It would have made a perfect photo. I almost grabbed my phone, but I didn't. This time I just enjoyed the view, keeping pace with Mom so that she could finish her route without stopping.

When we returned, little Bonbon was hanging around the *pâtisserie* door, waiting for dinner, just as she had been for the last couple of nights.

Mom smiled. "Hello, little dog," she said, extending her hand, but Bonbon backed away, regarding her suspiciously.

"She has a name now," I said.

"Oh?"

"Bonbon."

"That's really cute," Mom said, keeping her hand outstretched. Soon, Bonbon inched closer again, sniffed her hand, and began to wag her little tail. Then she let Mom pet her head and back. "You like that, don't you?" Mom said sweetly.

"Stay here, Mom. I'll be right back," I said and then hurried inside.

When I returned with a bowl of dog food, I set it down in front of Bonbon. "Here you go!"

She wolfed down her food, and then she nudged the palm of my hand, as if to say "Thanks."

Mom watched the two of us thoughtfully. Then she said, "Grace, remember that just because you name her—and feed her—doesn't mean we can bring her home."

"I know." I sighed heavily.

Mom went on. "And I still can't help wondering, sweetie, if the most responsible thing to do is to call the animal shelter here and get her off the street."

I jumped up. "But Mom, you heard Aunt Sophie— she might be put down!"

Mom reached for my hand. "Or," she said gently, "she might be reconnected with her owners, or find a new home."

"Might," I repeated sadly. "I don't like that word."

Mom rubbed my back. "I know. I'm sorry." Then she changed her tone. "But Grace, one thing's for sure: You've shown me that you can be very responsible. This stray is lucky to have you caring for her, at least until she finds a home."

Mom was complimenting me, but I felt a big lump in my throat. Bonbon looked up at me, her eyes so round and so dear. I wanted to cry. Instead, I pulled out my phone so that I could capture that sweet face and this moment. How many more would we have together?

Click!

Long after Mom went in for a shower, I sat beside Bonbon. I worried about what would happen to her when I left. Colette couldn't take her in. Sylvie couldn't either. There had to be *somebody* who could give her a home.

The Puppet Show
Chapter 10

*T*he night was still and warm. As Sylvie stretched across her bed and read a book, I sat on my mattress and updated my blog.

The window to the street was open, but our floor fan drowned out most of the sounds from the outdoor cafés and helped cool us down.

I posted a photo of Bonbon with the caption: *My new four-legged friend.*

By the time I'd posted a few other images, Ella had posted a message responding to my Bonbon photo:

Ella: *Soooo cute! Maddy's here with me. We both love your little friend.*

I did a quick mental calculation. Nine at night in Paris meant three in the afternoon at home. I pictured my friends sitting side by side at Ella's family computer in her living room. They seemed close right now, as I wrote to them, and yet terribly far away.

Me: *I do too! She's adorable.*

Ella: *Can you fly her home for us??? Ha!*

Me: *Wish I could! But my mom won't let me. : {*

Ella: *Too bad.*

I quickly changed the subject.

Me: *Hey, speaking of dogs, how's it going with your business?*

Ella: *Maddy and I are drumming up customers! We just added Dr. Mueller and his wife. They want us to walk their big dog, Tornado, every afternoon at four. Woohoo!*

A pang of jealousy wedged itself under my ribs. I wanted to be happy for my friends—I really did. But I felt so left out. I made myself type anyway.

Me: *Good for you!*

I next posted photos from my morning bike ride. Behind glass windows lay neat rows of treats of every size and color: round and square, triangular and rectangular, topped or filled with chocolate, strawberry, raspberry, blueberry, or mango.

For captions, I wrote:

Sure, Paris is known for its Eiffel Tower and Notre Dame, for berets and baguettes, for fashionable women walking little dogs. And all that's here. And more! But what do I LOVE? The pâtisseries! The boulangeries! No wonder my aunt came here and stayed . . .

Ella: *LOL! You're so weird! Don't get any funny ideas. You can't stay. We miss you here!*

I think I smiled from ear to ear when I read that line. I glanced over at Sylvie, to see if she'd caught me. But she was deep into her reading.

The Puppet Show

Me: *Miss you too—lots! I can't wait to share some new recipes with you two. I'm learning more each day at my uncle's bakery.*

Ella: *Fun!*

We chatted back and forth about where they'd been swimming and about my singing along with street musicians. But I felt a huge yawn coming on. I was definitely now on Paris time. I signed off.

Me: *Bedtime here. Bonsoir!*

Just then, a golden paw appeared beneath the bedroom door. It swished left and right, as if fishing for something.

I pulled the bookmark out of my travel guide and dangled the tassel near the crack under the door. Napoléon batted at it instantly, held it like a prize beneath his paw, and then let it go. Then he scratched at the door.

When I opened it, he strolled in. He leaped up onto Sylvie's bed and stretched out beside her. Not even the fan could drown out his happy purring.

I lay back on my own bed and sighed, wishing I had a pet to curl up beside me.

I scrolled down to the photo I'd posted of Bonbon. Her sweet black eyes stared back at me, as if trying to tell me something important.

My heart twisted.

I whispered beneath my breath, "I'd take you home, Bonbon—if only I could."

Geraniums bloomed bright red on the tiny balcony off the kitchen and living area. Classical music filled the room. Sylvie and I took turns holding Lily on the couch.

Sylvie sat with pillows on either side of her and held Lily in the crook of her arm. We talked *bébé* talk. And little Lily's tiny lips moved and almost smiled in response.

"Such a beautiful little girl!" I said as her tiny fingers wrapped around my forefinger.

"Quel beau bébé!" Sylvie would say, and Lily would

give her another adoring look that warmed me to my toes. With each passing day, I was feeling more a part of this family, despite our language barrier. One thing was certain: Neither Sylvie nor I had any trouble understanding little Lily's language.

One Sunday after Lily's nap, we joined Mom and Aunt Sophie on a walk to the Luxembourg Gardens. It was our first real outing all together, and I prided myself on recognizing a few landmarks, including the fountain with the lions. Things were becoming more familiar for me, but I still didn't want to be left on my own to find my way!

Beyond the gate, the gardens stretched on forever. I made a note of a few "rules" I wanted to post later on my blog:

- *Don't walk or play on the perfectly manicured grass.*
- *Do sail the little remote-controlled sailboats across the round pond.*
- *Do race go-carts down the long path—twice. I pedaled a red one first, and then a yellow!*

On the playground, Sylvie and I scaled the

miniature Eiffel Tower made with bungee cords. We were climbing the cords almost to the top when we heard the bells.

Cling, clang! Cling, clang!

Outside the squat nearby building, a man with a round face clanged a bell. His dark jacket stretched over his middle as he swung the handbell up and down.

Cling, clang! Cling, clang!

Kids around us slid down slide chutes and scurried off wooden ladders and platforms, as if the Pied Piper were calling to them. Parents left benches and gathered up toddlers, and soon Sylvie and I were waiting in line, heading for the building with the sign: *Les Marionettes.* A puppet show!

Most of the kids were younger (I guessed around four or five years old), but that gave me confidence. I'd been picking up more French every day, so surely I could understand a puppet show put on for little kids.

Aunt Sophie said to me, "Three Little Pigs, Grace."

"Good," I said with a smile. "Something I know."

Inside, rows of chairs and benches faced the curtained stage and a hum of chatter filled the air. Pictures of puppet characters lined the walls. The cat with a floppy hat must be Puss in Boots. The long-nosed character was Pinocchio. And I also saw pictures of Snow White and Captain Hook.

Mom sat in back with Aunt Sophie and Baby Lily, just in case she started to cry and they needed to make a quick exit. But Sylvie and I headed for the middle seats.

When the theater darkened and lights went up onstage, the audience grew silent. But the moment pig puppets dressed in jackets and trousers popped up, the audience broke into applause and cheers. An electric charge of excitement filled the room, and I clapped along to the music, glancing at Sylvie and sharing a quick smile. She'd probably been coming to this theater for as long as she could remember.

As the puppets began speaking, I settled in and focused, waiting for their words to become clear and take on meaning for me. They began asking the audience questions, and the littlest kids sitting in the front row responded.

The questions the puppets asked started with *quoi, pourquoi,* or *qui,* which meant *what, why,* and *who.*

I got that much, and I heard the word *travail*.
Work.

Those three little pigs were good workers, with their houses made of straw, wood, and bricks. But I only got that much because I already knew the story.

As the pig puppets danced and sang, the children squealed with delight and cheered them on.

A hush fell whenever the wolf appeared.

I tried really, really hard to understand the words. I knew the basic story, of course, but this version had twists and turns that I didn't expect. And I understood only a word here and a word there.

Travail.

Work. Work. Work.

Here's what I did understand: Learning French was much more work than I'd thought it would be. I sank slowly in my chair. I'd expected to be speaking French and understanding it easily by this time in my visit. Yet I still understood so little!

I felt like an outsider, like someone who can't read in a world of readers. Instead of being part of the audience as it chimed in and cheered and clapped, I felt totally left out. I just wanted the play to end.

When the lights finally came up and the audience cheered for the puppet master, the very man who had been ringing the bell outside, I breathed a sigh of relief and clapped along with the others.

But as parents and children rose and filed out, I stayed seated and confessed to Sylvie, "I didn't understand a word! Well, maybe two or three."

She nodded. "Like English for me," she said, looking at her lap. *"Très difficile!"*

"Very difficult," I translated.

She nodded, her eyes wide. *"Oui!"*

I exhaled deeply. If English was difficult for Sylvie, why did I think I could learn her language overnight? Maybe because at home, I was used to getting good grades and doing pretty well at most things I tried. I wasn't used to feeling so . . . stupid. But I knew that I wasn't stupid—and that Sylvie probably felt the same way whenever I used English, expecting her to understand. In some ways, we had much more in common than I'd realized.

I pulled out my dictionary and looked up the French word for cousin. To my surprise, it listed the same spelling: *cousin.*

I showed it to her. "Cousin," I said. "We spell it the same way!"

She smiled. "*Oui!* Boy cousin. Same. But girl *cousine* . . ." She pointed to me and then to herself.

At first I didn't get it. "Oh, you add an *e* at the end for female. I get it."

Sylvie nodded, happy that I had understood her. We stood up, nearly the last ones to leave, and headed up the aisle toward the red sign with the word: *SORTIE.*

"Ah," I said. "Exit.'"

"Exit," Sylvie repeated, following my gaze. Then she linked her arm in mine and said, "We cousins."

"*Oui,*" I replied, squeezing her arm. "Our mothers are sisters."

She translated. *"Nos mères sont soeurs."*

A wave of unexpected happiness floated over me. "Being your cousin makes me want to learn French!" I said.

Sylvie hesitated, cocking her head for a moment, but after I repeated my wish slowly, she grinned. *"Moi aussi,"* Sylvie said brightly as we stepped outside into the sunshine. She pointed to her chest. *"Anglais!"*

"You, too. English?" I translated.

"Oui, oui!"

Arm in arm, we joined Mom and Aunt Sophie as they chatted in the cool shade of a towering tree. It looked familiar to me, with its bark peeled away in large patches, revealing light gray, light green, and white. It looked just like a tree in our backyard at home. I looked up at its leaves, sheltering us from the hot sun. They looked sort of like maple leaves, and from them hung little clusters of acorn-like balls.

As Aunt Sophie carefully put a sleeping Lily into the stroller, I touched the tree with the flat of my hand. *"Qu'est ce que c'est?"* I asked.

"C'est un arbre," Sylvie replied.

"Arbre. Tree. Yes," I said, "but, I mean, what kind of tree?"

She didn't seem to understand.

Aunt Sophie said something in French to Sylvie, who nodded.

"Ahh," Sylvie said, looking from her stepmom to me. *"C'est un platane,* Grace!"

"At home, you call it a *sycamore,*" explained Aunt Sophie. "A sycamore tree."

"Sick is more!" Sylvie repeated with confidence.

I couldn't hold back a giggle. "No, not 'sick is more.' It's 'sic-a-more,'" I said, trying to help. Then I started off a giggle session with Sylvie that woke up Lily and started her crying.

We both had so much to learn!

A block before we reached the *pâtisserie*, Sylvie and I raced ahead of our mothers. She was fast, even if she was a year younger! We rounded the corner, exactly in stride with each other, and I knew we were both expecting to see Bonbon.

But she wasn't sitting at the back door.

She wasn't there wagging her tail, ready for her bowl of dog food. And her water bowl was still full.

"Where is she?" I asked, looking up and down the street.

"Bonbon!" Sylvie called.

But the street, cooling slightly in the late-afternoon shadows, didn't show any sign of a little wandering dog. My stomach twisted. Where was she?

That evening, Mom said we'd babysit so that Uncle Bernard, Aunt Sophie, and Sylvie could go see Sylvie's grandfather, who was living alone. The fresh air during our afternoon walk must have been just what little Lily needed, because she hadn't made a peep from her bassinet in over an hour.

Mom and I both sat on the couch, and I leaned into her shoulder as she read *Motivating Students, One Book at a Time*. I turned pages in Sylvie's old picture books, all in French. A few words and phrases seemed to make sense.

But when I turned to the page with a dog on it, I broke the silence and said, "Mom, can you call some-one? Can you see if Bonbon's in an animal shelter somewhere? Please? I'm worried sick. Maybe she got hit by a car. Or she's sick and needs help, or—"

"Or found her way home," Mom said.

I half-snorted in frustration.

"Honey," she said, putting down her book and placing her hand on mine. "I know you're worried about losing Bonbon, but you have to remember that she was never yours to begin with."

I knew Mom was right, but I didn't want to hear it. I closed my eyes tightly, hoping that she was also right about Bonbon finding her way home. I tried to picture Bonbon wandering the streets of Paris, traveling farther from the city to find her owners. She was too nice a dog not to have had them—once. She'd be tired when she got there, and hungry and thirsty. I pictured her owners greeting her at the door in tears and throwing their arms around her, welcoming her home.

It helped, but only a little.

And then I remembered Mom's words a few days back.

"Mom, did you call and have her picked up by the authorities, like Uncle Bernard said we should?" A hot flame tickled the back of my throat.

At first Mom didn't answer, and the fire wafted, shooting higher.

"Oh no! Mom, you didn't!"

She set her book down firmly. "No, Grace. I did not."

My voice grew smaller. "Okay. Sorry, I just worried—"

"I know." She gazed off toward the window and then met my eyes. "I'll tell you what. I'll have your aunt help me make a few calls to see if we can learn anything about Bonbon. I'm doubtful, Grace, but maybe making the calls would help put your mind at ease."

I swallowed hard and nodded, and then I hugged her as tightly as I could.

A shower can't cure every problem, but it helps. As I towel-dried my hair in the bathroom, I gazed at the bold yellow, red, and blue wall tiles. Normally they cheered me up, but not tonight. I slipped into my comfy PJ's, nestled back on the couch beside Mom, and asked her if I could go online.

I posted photos from our afternoon at the Luxembourg Gardens: Sylvie and me in go-carts, beside our little sailboats, and leaning over the edge of a garden fountain and pool. Then I sent off a quick e-mail to Maddy:

Bonbon is gone! She didn't show up for her dinner.

It didn't take long to hear back.

Maddy: *Too bad about Bonbon! Maybe she'll show up tomorrow. She's a stray. She probably has a mind of her own.*

Me: *Hope so. Hey, how's your dog-walking business?*

Maddy: *Not great. After Tornado ran off with his leash and the owners went crazy with worry, we backed off the dog-walking business. At least for now.*

Me: *What?! Did they get their dog back?*

Maddy: *Yesssss. After about six hours of his being lost. The Muellers were NOT happy about it. But how were we supposed to know that he went into someone's house for a long visit?*

Me: *Whose house?*

Maddy: *A neighbor of theirs—an older lady. She must have fed him like a whole casserole and he napped the hours away. That's why he didn't come when we called him. When she let him out, he just walked home.*

Me: *Too bad.*

Maddy: *But maybe that's exactly what happened to your little stray. Bet you'll see her tomorrow!*

Me: *Yeah. Hope so!*

Maddy: *Are you having an amazing time there? You're so lucky!*

Me: *Yeah. It's good. And hey, I'm sorry about your business not working. Maybe when I get home we can brainstorm for ways to make it work better—or try some other business idea.*

But as I wrote that line about being "sorry," part of me actually felt glad, since I wasn't included in Maddy and Ella's dog-walking plans anyway. And part of me felt bad that I felt glad that their business hadn't taken off. Friends are supposed to be happy for their friends when they're happy, and sad when they're sad, right? But sometimes . . . friendship isn't so simple.

To the Palace

Chapter 11

One afternoon, "all us girls," as Mom said, were hanging out on Aunt Sophie's bed, admiring Lily, who had just had a bath. Aunt Sophie smoothed Lily with lotion and then dressed her in a soft cotton dress.

Looking at Lily, Sylvie said something in French and then turned to her mom.

"You want me to translate?" Aunt Sophie asked as she swaddled Lily in a pink baby blanket.

Sylvie nodded and then glanced at me. I wondered what she had to say, because from the almost-teary expression on her face, it seemed sort of serious. Was she upset with me about something?

But Aunt Sophie's smile reassured me. "Sylvie wants you to know, Grace, that before you came to visit, she felt a little lost. She was missing her *grand-mère* and worried about a baby coming. She didn't know where she would fit in."

Sylvie added a few more words in French, and Aunt Sophie translated. "She wants you to know that now she can't imagine her life without Lily—or without *you*."

Sylvie looked at me and smiled.

My heart swelled, and I beamed back. "*Merci beaucoup,* Sylvie," I said. "I am happy to be here, too."

At the *pâtisserie,* Colette seemed to wear a new apron every few days. Today's *tablier du jour*—apron of the day—was pale blue with a jillion red pockets.

"I love your aprons," I said, wondering how she could afford to own so many. But she must have read my mind.

"I like . . . how you say?" She mimed stitching, weaving a needle in and out of imaginary fabric.

"You like to sew. No wonder you have so many!"

She nodded and then offered sweetly, "Do you want one, Grace? I sew you one?"

I grinned. "Sure!"

Sylvie seemed to piece together the conversation

as she edged in closer. Then Colette spoke to Sylvie in French.

"*Oui, oui,*" Sylvie replied with a big smile. Was she getting an apron, too? I hoped so!

That afternoon, when I checked my online calendar, I was shocked. How could I have just two weeks left in Paris? Each day had dragged by at first, but now the days flew by and I wanted to slow them down. I wanted to soak up every moment here in Paris, and yet I couldn't stop part of my brain from thinking about being home, too, and starting a business with my friends. Something tickled at the back of my mind . . .

Aprons.

Colette had given me the perfect business idea! My friends and I could make and sell aprons.

I went online and shot off the idea to Ella and Maddy.

But that night, the reply that came back was brief:

Ella: *Good idea, but Maddy and I don't have sewing machines—or know how to sew. Let's keep thinking . . . Hey, Maddy's here! She slept over last night.*

My mood took a sudden nosedive, maybe because Ella had shot down my business idea, or maybe because my friends were having another fun sleepover—without me. Now that I was nearing the end of my trip, I worried again: *What if everything has changed between me and my friends by the time I go home?*

This time, though, I chased away the thought and told myself, *Think. You just need to come up with a new business idea that you can ALL be a part of when you get back.* But what? Trying to get all of us to agree on something wouldn't be easy, but I was determined. While here, I would be looking for ideas. I would brainstorm, just as Grandpa had told me to do at the start of summer.

And then it hit me. *Grandma and Grandpa!* They run a business. Why not ask for some advice about a business that my friends and I could run back home?

I pulled out a stack of postcards I'd been collecting and started to write one out to Grandma and Grandpa. But this was something I wanted an answer to right away, so I typed my message again in an e-mail:

Dear Grandma and Grandpa,
I am finally learning to bake and cook a little in the pâtisserie.

And Lily is getting cuter every day!

Remember when I asked about starting a business? I still want to find an idea to try with my friends. Can you give me some advice? As soon as you possibly can???

Miss and love you!

Grace

Sylvie, who carried Napoléon on her shoulder, plopped down beside me on the couch. Napoléon's purring sounded like the diesel train back home that winds through the Blackstone Valley. When I was younger and Grandma and I'd had "tea parties" with her fine china, the train had often passed on the tracks nearby, jiggling our cups and saucers. The memory stuck in my throat.

I missed Grandma and Grandpa.

Sylvie pointed to the postcard I had written. *"Grand-mère? Grand-père?"* she asked.

"Oui," I replied, still holding back tears. But then I thought of Sylvie's French grandma who had died a short time ago—the grandma Sylvie had been close to. I couldn't imagine not having my grandparents around.

Then a brighter thought struck: My grandparents

were *Sylvie's* new grandparents, too. She'd met them briefly in the States when her dad and stepmom got married, but she didn't really know them . . . *yet*.

Maybe I could help change that. If Sylvie could get to know her grandparents in the States, maybe that would help fill some of the empty space she must feel for her French grandma.

I held out a different postcard to Sylvie. *"Veux-tu . . ."* I mimed writing on the postcard and said, "You write to new *grand-mère? Grand-père?"*

Her brown eyes widened as she smiled. *"Oui! Oui!"*

With Aunt Sophie's help, Sylvie sat at the table and wrote her postcard in English. Then she read it aloud to me in her French accent:

Dear Grand-mère and Grand-père,
Bonjour! You must see your new grandbaby! I love having my new sister, Lilou. We call her Lily. And we have a cat we call Napoléon. Someday we see each other again!
Love,
Sylvie

Then I read my postcard aloud to her, with
Aunt Sophie translating.

Sylvie said something to her stepmom, who relayed
it to me. "Grace, about trying to find a business idea,
Sylvie says she wants to help you."

I looked at Sylvie. "Yes! I help you!" she said happily.

"Really?" I said. "That'd be great, Sylvie." Looking
for business ideas would be something fun that she
and I could do together. Besides, at this point, I could
use all the help I could get!

To keep Mom company on her long run early the
next morning, Sylvie and I biked after her.

First stop, however: mail our postcards. Aunt Sophie
had made sure we added *Etats-Unis* in big letters for
"United States" on each postcard. And because she had
stamps on hand, our task was easy. All we had to do
was keep an eye out for one of the many yellow letter
boxes marked *La Poste*. We found one just two blocks
from the apartment, popped our postcards inside, and
continued on our way. *Voilà!*

As we passed a dog walker, I thought of Bonbon. Mom hadn't been able to find out any information about her yet. I tried not to worry, but I couldn't help scanning the streets for her everywhere we went.

There were lots of dog walkers. I wondered for a moment if I could find a way to help Ella and Maddy improve their dog-walking business. Or was there an even better business idea out there for all of us?

Along with the dog walkers, the streets were crowded with people walking, jogging, and biking. So many of them appeared trim and fit.

"Mom," I said as we paused at a light, "with all the pastries and amazing food, I'm surprised more French people aren't overweight."

Mom chuckled. "It's all about balance," she said in between deep breaths, "and staying active. Plus, have you noticed that the French don't snack much?"

"Except at about four o'clock," I said. "That's when Sylvie and I always have a snack." Aunt Sophie had a name for it, that time in the late afternoon when she pulled out a piece of cake or maybe slices of bread with jam or chocolate. "What's that afternoon snack called?" I asked Sylvie as she biked up beside me.

She stared at me intently, as if piecing my words together. "Snack," she repeated slowly. Then she said, "Ah, *le goûter*?"

That was it! "*Merci*, Sylvie."

She smiled, seeming pleased with herself.

Not long after, as we followed Mom along the Seine, an all-in-one bike-cab passed us. The bicyclist pedaled hard, carrying a passenger seated in the sheltered cab behind him. A sign on the back of the cab read *You Can Start Your Own Pedi-Cab Business!*

"Grace!" Sylvie said, pointing to the pedicab as it passed. "Business—you?"

"Yes!" I said, pulling to a stop. I whipped out my phone. *Click!*

But as I pedaled fast to catch up to Mom and Sylvie, I tried to actually imagine operating a pedicab at home. Maybe I could pedal one empty, but what if an adult got in and needed a ride? I pictured myself huffing and puffing up a long, steep hill and losing momentum. Down we'd slide to the bottom of the hill.

"*Très difficile!*" I called to Sylvie.

"Yes," she replied with a grimace. She must have been playing it out in her mind, too.

⌒ To the Palace ⌒

Mom rounded a corner, and we headed across a bridge toward the Right Bank. On the bridge, a mime was covered in sparkling silver. He swept a small pile of coins in front of his push broom and stopped for tourists who wanted to take photos of him—or beside him. There was one way to make a little money!

Click!

I thought of how I had stepped out of my comfort zone to sing along with Colette and Sylvie on the bridge that day. I'd done it! But I just couldn't quite see me and my friends dressing up and miming on the streets back home.

Luckily, other new ideas popped up along every block.

Two hours later, we made it back to the apartment. Mom's face was blotchy red, and Aunt Sophie insisted she drink lots of water. I was tired, too, but my mind was racing. There were way too many ideas out there!

I posted images on my blog of business ideas, starting with the street mime. I posted photos of a woman selling grilled corn, a teenager with a table of bracelets made of braided fabric, a man at a street booth filled with candies, and artists selling their paintings along the Seine. They all looked like they were having fun.

Help!

I hoped to get an e-mail back from Grandma and Grandpa soon. I needed some advice, ASAP!

As the first week of August approached, I learned that August is the month when many Parisians go on holiday and leave the city for the countryside. Uncle Bernard said, "We will close the shop for a couple of days. Be tourists!"

As Lily "figured out her nights"—or in other words, started sleeping more at night—everyone seemed happier. Mom was back to a regular running schedule, Aunt Sophie was looking more rested and doing more each day, and Uncle Bernard started talking about holiday plans and all we'd see and do before Mom and I went back to the States.

I was feeling part of this French family at last—just as it was almost time to go!

On August first, the *pâtisserie* would close up and Colette's internship would end. So on her last day, she produced two packages from behind her back. "Open, *s'il te plaît*," she said to me and to Sylvie.

We unwrapped the packages and held up aprons with pink satin ribbons. Mine was black with pink polka dots and Sylvie's was orange with pink polka dots. We tried them on, beaming.

Sylvie wrapped her arms around Colette's waist. "*Merci*, Colette!"

Before I could do the same, Colette pulled something from her pocket and held it clasped in her hand. "I found this for you, Grace."

It was a charm of a little dog with upright ears and short legs. "A French bulldog," she said.

"Bonbon!" I said, wanting to cry but smiling at the same time. "Thank you soooo much, Colette!"

I didn't know where Bonbon was, but at least I'd have the charm as a memory of her—something I could carry with me always. I hugged Colette hard and then added the charm to my nearly full bracelet, which now held the Eiffel Tower, a camera, a postcard, a *macaron*, and a silver mixing bowl—tiny treasures I'd found on my trip.

I hated to say good-bye when I felt as if I was just

starting to get to know Colette. But the bakers and Uncle Bernard had a surprise for her, too: a triple-layered cake. It was delicious!

Before she left that day, she kissed us each on the top of our heads. And then, as I watched her bike away, I let the tears come.

In the sleepy hours of early morning, we left the cobblestone streets of Paris in a rental car for the widening roads of the green countryside. The Palace of *Versailles* was less than an hour's drive outside of Paris, but my aunt and uncle wanted to get an early start to beat the crowds and arrive before the day heated up.

Aunt Sophie was driving, with Mom sitting beside her in front. Aunt Sophie insisted on driving, because she'd driven for years in the States before coming to Paris. Uncle Bernard, like many Parisians, hadn't spent as much time behind the wheel. Instead, he sat in the middle seat beside Lily's infant seat. And Lily? She was happily making bubbles with her spit.

As we traveled along, Mom turned around and

asked, "Sylvie, have you been to Versailles?"

"*Non,*" said Sylvie, sitting beside me way in the back.

Good! I thought. For once, we'll both be seeing something new together.

Because we'd left Paris so early, we reached the palace right when it was opening and didn't have to wait in line for our tour. Our guide, a young woman in ballet shoes and a swirling skirt, explained that King Louis the Fourteenth had built the palace far away from Paris because when he was a boy in the city, there had been attempts on his life. So he turned swampland into the palace grounds. "About thirty-seven thousand acres were cleared to make room for a walkway, tree-lined terraces, and thousands of flowering plants," she said. "At one point, there were fourteen hundred fountains and four hundred pieces of sculpture. King Louis the Fourteenth was a man full of ideas."

Mom leaned down to whisper in my ear, "Sounds like someone else I know."

I grinned as we followed our guide to the next room.

"Construction," the guide continued, "went on for years and took more than thirty-six thousand workers.

But when it was complete, the palace could accommodate up to five thousand people, including servants."

Thirty-six thousand workers? I couldn't help thinking that if I ever managed to turn an idea into a business, I'd start with just three workers: Ella, Maddy, and me.

Following our guide, we walked and walked. The palace seemed to stretch on forever. I craned my neck at gilded ceilings, admired wall-size paintings, and marveled at the ornate chairs, tables, and sofas. As long as I didn't use a flash, I was allowed to take photos at every chance.

When our guide pointed out a hidden passageway between rooms, disguised by bookcases, I thought of Ella. She loved mysteries!

Click!

At the end of the palace tour, we headed outside under a mid-morning sun. The grounds stretched on and on with canals, massive fountains, mazes of green hedges, and dazzling displays of flowers. Sylvie and I followed along at our own pace after the adults. I was feeling a little sleepy after getting up so early. Lily had it made, I thought, sleeping away against Uncle Bernard's chest in the baby carrier.

Mom slowed down and waited for us to catch up.

"Grace," Mom said, "remember when we celebrated Bastille Day a couple of weeks ago?"

I nodded. I remembered France's independence day well. It was the day Sylvie and I had gone for ice cream, and I had been brave enough to stand up and sing with her and Colette. I sighed. So much had happened since then. It seemed so long ago!

"During the revolution, an angry mob stormed this palace—right here at Versailles."

I glanced around me and let it all sink in. History was so much more interesting out here, where I was standing on the same ground where the revolution had taken place. I shuddered, thinking of the king and queen who had lost their heads. "I'm glad we're visiting *after* their revolution," I said. "Not during."

Sylvie nodded solemnly, and I wondered how much of that she'd understood.

When we reached the village that Marie Antoinette had created so that she could escape palace life during her reign here, I found myself getting homesick. The little farm with stone buildings, ponds, and a water mill reminded me of the Blackstone Valley, with its rolling fields, dense thickets, and old brick mills.

We all stopped to sit in the grass beside a pond.

Two majestic swans, with orange bills trimmed black, preened their ivory feathers as they floated. They seemed totally unconcerned that we were there watching them.

A wave of silliness came over me, and I spoke in a grand voice and extended my hand toward them with a flourish. "Royal swans," I said.

"*Cygnes royaux,*" Sylvie said, imitating me and gesturing, as if she were ushering in the king and queen.

"Watch your heads," I advised them.

Mom smiled at my joke.

We lingered a little longer, watching the swans, who in their own way were just as beautiful as everything else at the palace. My mind drifted, thinking about how hard it would be to update my blog about Versailles. There's just so much to say—where would I start? Maybe I'd say this:

• *If you close your eyes, you can almost imagine royal carriages, horses, lords, and ladies arriving at the gates of gold and entering the vast cobblestone court.*

• *King Louis XIV (the 14th) was called the Sun King, because the court revolved around him—until the revolution started in 1789. Then later, it was King Louis XVI (the 16th) and the queen who lost their heads.*

• *Benjamin Franklin went to France and got a treaty signed that made the French and Americans friends (allies). Then the French sent soldiers, sailors, money, and ships to America. We probably wouldn't have won our independence without aid from the French!*

That night, I posted a few photos from Versailles on my blog. My caption read: *The power of an idea—and a whole lot of gold.*

Just as I was logging out, I heard the *ding* of an incoming e-mail. It was from Grandma and Grandpa. Finally! And Grandpa definitely had some good advice about being in business:

Number 1: *Do what you love. (What gets you excited and gives you energy?)*

Number 2: *Make it your own! (How can you stand out and make your product unique?)*

I gazed out the open bedroom window, listening to someone playing a mandolin. Sylvie was already sleeping, her breaths coming soft and slow. Napoléon curled up in the crook of her legs, watching me.

I thought about Grandpa's advice: *Do what you love.*

I looked over at Napoléon. Sylvie loved her cat and spent time with him every day.

And I loved Bonbon. I wanted a dog—I wanted her. But that was different. Grandpa didn't say *Get what you love.* He said *Do what you love.*

Dad had hobbies he loved, whether it was making unusual birdhouses, fixing up the old stone wall, or scraping and waxing his skis. Mom was energized by running and working toward her first half marathon. And besides fooling around on the piano, Josh loved anything related to bikes—riding them, reading about them, and fixing them.

What did I love to do? That was easy. Ever since I can remember, I've loved baking: creating something out of nothing, or at least turning simple ingredients into something surprising and delicious. And all the while here in Paris, the thing that had tickled me most? The pastries—the special French creations—displayed in every *pâtisserie* case and window. No wonder most of my blog photos were now of "art you can eat."

But . . . I dropped back down to my mattress.

Baking couldn't work. Not for a business with Maddy and Ella. In June, when I'd first suggested selling baked goods as a business idea, they hadn't jumped on the idea. They'd more like stomped on it.

Still . . . what if I could find a way to make baking my own? How could I make it stand out? And if I could make it unique, as Grandpa had said to do . . . If I could prove I had a good idea, could I then convince my friends to join me, too?

I didn't know the answers. Not yet. But when I closed my eyes, a hum of excitement and energy buzzed inside me!

A Sweet Surprise
Chapter 12

*A*s we sat around the breakfast table, I felt torn between two worlds.

Two *homes.*

How could I fly home tomorrow without knowing when I'd ever see Sylvie, Lily, and my aunt and uncle again? I buttered my *croissant* and smothered it with apricot jam, afraid it might stick in my throat. I took a big drink of orange juice, and a big breath. One day left. A day of fun and exploring. I was not going to cry.

The flaky, buttery *croissant* melted in my mouth. I closed my eyes, trying to memorize the taste.

As Uncle Bernard and Mom discussed flight schedules and what time we'd need to leave for the airport tomorrow, I glanced around the table.

After five whole weeks, I'd come to know everyone's footsteps through the apartment. I knew who was up

early and first to fill the kettle with water and turn on
the stove with a *click*. I knew who drank tea and who
drank coffee, French-press style. I knew when Lily was
murmuring to herself in her bassinet that if her little
voice shifted and changed pitch, her crying would follow in about five seconds.

I knew that Sylvie talked in her sleep, often scolding
someone, which made me wake up and giggle.

And it's funny, but I knew *me* better, too. I knew
how to handle new things better than I'd ever dreamed
I could. I understood and spoke a little more French
every day. I could even create a few French treats.
And I'd learned that even if I don't always have a fully
"baked" plan, things still usually turn out okay.

That thought made me feel better. I drank my last
swig of orange juice, ready to get on with the day.

An hour later, we all boarded the subway, an amazing color-coded system that runs under Paris. Soon,
we arrived in the neighborhood of *Montmartre*. As we
climbed the steps toward daylight under fanciful green

ironwork and two glowing red lights, I felt as if we were stepping out of a dragon's mouth into sunlight. I knew that I couldn't capture that feeling in a photo, but I had to try.

Click!

Uncle Bernard lugged Lily's stroller, while Aunt Sophie now wore the baby carrier strapped to her front, with a sleeping Lily inside.

Last day, last day, last day, I kept reminding myself over and over in my head. But I just wasn't ready to leave tomorrow.

We strolled past a whole street of fabric shops with tables of fabric of every color, every texture. I wondered if Colette bought her fabric here. I would really miss her, and still couldn't believe how sweet it was of her to make Sylvie and me our polka-dotted aprons. I'd cherish mine and use it at home.

A tickle of excitement filled me. I was going home. I would turn my baking into a business—somehow! The energy from that idea helped. But I still felt a longing to stay, at least a few more days.

The streets wound their way to the base of a steep hill. Uncle Bernard pointed to its top, where a white stone church towered toward the sky. *"Voilà! Le Sacré-Coeur!"* he said. "The Sacred Heart of Montmartre."

It was a long climb up to this famous church. We had two choices: a zillion steps or a funnel-like tram called the funicular that zipped visitors right to the top.

Mom said, "We need the exercise. Let's do the steps."

Aunt Sophie agreed.

Sylvie and I looked at each other and rolled our eyes, and then we started climbing after them. Halfway up, my muscles burned, and we stopped to rest.

"C'est dur!" Sophie said. "It's hard!"

I agreed, but then it occurred to me that if Colette were with us, she'd make the climb fun by breaking into song. So I decided to give it a try.

"Frère Jacques, Frère Jacques . . ." I began singing.

Sylvie started in, too, turning the song into a round.

And then Mom joined us, and then Aunt Sophie, and finally even Uncle Bernard, who surprised me with his deep baritone voice.

Frère Jacques,
Frère Jacques,

Grace

Dormez-vous?
Dormez-vous?
Sonnez les matines.
Sonnez les matines.
Ding, dang, dong.
Ding, dang, dong.

We kept singing with each step upward, and I pictured monks rising early to ring the morning bells by pulling on the heavy ropes in the bell tower. Our voices harmonized and floated on the air, almost like the church bells that rang out so frequently over Paris. Uncle Bernard ended the round, his voice deep and full.

Before I knew it, we were at the top. The steps had flown by!

"That was fun!" Mom exclaimed. She was barely out of breath, but I gulped deep breaths to get my heartbeat back to normal.

Towering statues of horses and riders guarded the massive stone church. Before joining the line up yet more steps to tour inside, we wove our way past street merchants lined up at the base of the church. They were selling wooden puzzles, replicas of Sacré-Coeur, bracelets, postcards, and bookmarks.

Sylvie and I made our way to the stone wall and gazed down. Below us, the shops and cafés of Montmarte looked like dollhouses. And tomorrow, from my window seat on the plane, everything would get smaller and smaller until it all disappeared from view.

I wasn't ready!

"Sylvie," I said, "I wish you could come with me—*avec moi*—to the United States."

She blinked back tears. How I'd misread her big brown eyes when I first arrived. I had thought she hadn't wanted me here, when actually, she'd just been nervous about communicating with me in English. But her English had improved, right along with my French.

"Me too!" she said, but then gave her head a shake. "Big money. New *bébé*."

"*Oui*," I said. "I know."

We leaned into each other, shoulder to shoulder, and looked out over Paris. The city stretched into an endless maze of streets and buildings. Music drifted up from street musicians, and outdoor cafés brimmed with customers.

～ Grace ～

I suddenly realized what makes Paris more than just another city. It isn't the Eiffel Tower or the countless "locks of love" at the Pont des Arts. It's not even the history of the city, so much older than our own.

Paris is Paris because of its *people*.

Parisians seem to make the ordinary details extraordinary.

It's in every enthusiastic *Bonjour!* and *Au revoir!*

It's in perfectly made strawberry *tartes* and *pains au chocolat*.

It's in the way people take time to gather at outdoor cafés.

And it's in the music they play that lifts from subways and drifts down cobblestone streets.

I grabbed Sylvie's arm, startling her.

"*Quoi?* What?" she asked.

"Sylvie! I have it! I have it!"

She looked at my hands, as if I'd just found something incredibly valuable. And I had.

"What, Grace?" she asked.

"My business idea!"

Her eyes met mine, and she waited for me to go on.

"A Paris-style *pâtisserie*!" That hum of energy filled

me all over again. I explained to Sylvie how my friends and I could make beautiful French pastries and serve them with *je ne sais quoi*—that "I don't know what" that makes something special.

Sylvie beamed. *"C'est magnifique!"*

Just then, Uncle Bernard held up his camera. *"Les filles!* Girls!"

We faced his camera, with all of Paris behind us, linked arms, and smiled.

Click!

My alarm went off, signaling my very last day in Paris. I fumbled to turn off the buzzer in the predawn darkness. Luckily I had packed the night before, so I only had to get dressed.

After giving sleepy good-bye hugs to Aunt Sophie and Baby Lily, I followed Sylvie into the backseat of the rental car behind Mom and Uncle Bernard. Then we began zipping along the nearly empty roads of Paris.

Though Sylvie sat beside me, and there was so much I still wanted to say to her, I couldn't keep my eyes open. I quickly drifted off to sleep.

But when the car stopped, I straightened up.

We weren't at the airport.

Fields stretched into the distance, and the sun beamed down on a farmhouse with lavender shutters.

"Mom? Where are we?"

"I'll be right back!" she said as she hopped out of the car and hurried up to the farmhouse door. She knocked and soon disappeared inside.

I was confused. Was she doing some last-minute shopping before catching our plane? That seemed like terrible planning on her part. We'd been in Paris long enough to get anything she'd needed.

"Uncle Bernard?" I asked.

He looked at me and Sylvie and offered a mere shrug and a smile.

When the farmhouse door swung open again, a woman with a long white braid stepped outside with Mom. They exchanged a few words, and then Mom wheeled a green luggage case down the driveway toward the car. We had overpacked, and we probably needed an extra bag, but why pick up something here?

I leaned forward, elbows on my knees, trying

to make sense of what Mom was doing. Something unscheduled and last-minute—and on the way to the airport? This was so unlike her.

She opened my car door and I glanced out. Behind Mom, from the mesh end of the rolling case, two shiny eyes peered back at me.

It was *Bonbon.*

"Mom! How did you . . . ?"

She just smiled, put the travel case on the seat beside me, and then jumped back into the passenger seat up front.

The green nylon case wiggled and thumped.

"C'est Bonbon!" Sylvie exclaimed.

"Can I take her out?" I asked.

"Sure," Mom said.

I unzipped the opening. Bonbon climbed out and onto my lap. She kissed my cheek and wagged her whole body. She gave Sylvie a kiss, too, and then came back to my lap. She smelled freshly shampooed. Someone had clipped her nails and fastened a little bow to her collar.

"Bonbon, you look so sweet!" I said. "Mom, how did you know she was here?"

Mom explained. "I said I'd do some research, didn't I? Well, your aunt and I finally found her at a shelter and started the adoption process about a week ago. She was fostered at this little farm, until now."

Sylvie started giggling.

And then I figured it out. "Sylvie, she's yours now!" Part of me was a little sad that Bonbon couldn't be mine, but the other part of me was so happy for Sylvie—and for Bonbon, who would have a forever home at last.

Sylvie grinned, but she shook her head back and forth.

"Grace," Mom said, "you watched out for this little dog and used your own money to keep her fed. You've proven how responsible you can be with a dog. So we had Bonbon examined by a veterinarian, who gave us her health certificate so that she could travel to the States. And I checked with the airline, and she's small enough to ride in a dog carrier with you on the plane. So, Grace, what do you say? Do you want to bring her home?"

Hot tears rushed to my eyes and fell down my cheeks. I didn't bother to wipe them away. I looked from Mom to Sylvie, who couldn't keep from smiling, and then back to Bonbon with her pirate patch and upright ears.

Mom turned to me, waiting for an answer.

I placed my hands around Bonbon's sweet face and looked into her black eyes. More than once, she'd tried to tell me what she needed.

Now at last I could answer her—and Mom.

"Want to?" I said in disbelief. "Oh, yes! *Oui, oui!*"

Glossary of French Words

Aimes-tu la glace? *(em-tew lah glahss)*—Do you like ice cream?

Allez donc vous prendre une glace? *(ah-lay dohnk voo prahn-druh ewn glahss)*—Why don't you go have an ice cream?

amandine *(ah-mahn-deen)*—a tart made with almonds, eggs, flour, butter, and sugar

anglais *(ahn-gleh)*—English

Arrêtez-vous! *(ah-reh-tay-voo)*—Stop!

arrondissement *(ah-rohn-deess-mahn)*—neighborhood or district

au revoir *(oh ruh-vwar)*—good-bye

avec moi *(ah-vek mwah)*—with me

Avez-vous faim? *(ah-vay-voo fam)*—Are you hungry?

baguette *(bah-get)*—a long, thin loaf of French bread

bébé *(bay-bay)*—baby

béret *(bay-reh)*—a round hat with a tight band around the head and a flat, loose top

Berthillon *(behr-tee-yohn)*—a famous ice cream shop in Paris

bon *(bohn)*—good

bon appétit *(bohn ah-pay-tee)*—good appetite; enjoy your meal

bonbon au chocolat *(bohn-bohn oh sho-ko-lah)*—candy with a soft center and a chocolate outer shell bonjour *(bohn-zhoor)*—hello

bonsoir *(bohn-swar)*—good evening

bon voyage *(bohn vwah-yazh)*—safe journey

boulangerie *(boo-lahn-zhuh-ree)*—a French bakery that specializes in breads and may serve lunch, too

Café de Flore *(kah-fay duh flohr)*—a famous café in Paris

c'est *(say)*—it's

C'est beau! *(say boh)*—It's beautiful!

C'est dommage! *(say doh-mahzh)*—It's a pity!

C'est dur! *(say dyewr)*—It's hard!

C'est magnifique *(say mah-nyee-feek)*—It's beautiful, magnificent

chaussons aux pommes *(shoh-sohn oh pum)*—apple turnovers

Comment vas-tu? *(koh-mahn vah-tew)*—How are you?

cousin *(koo-zehn)*—male cousin

cousine *(koo-zeen)*—female cousin

crème brûlée *(krem broo-lay)*—a sweet dessert made of custard with a caramelized top

croissant *(kwa-sahn)*—a flaky crescent-shaped roll

croque-monsieur *(krohk-muh-syuh)*—a grilled cheese sandwich with ham

cygnes royaux *(see-nyuh roh-yoh)*—royal swans

Dormez-vous? *(dor-may voo)*—Are you sleeping?

éclair *(ay-klehr)*—a long pastry filled with whipped or sweet cream, often topped with chocolate

éclair au café *(ay-klehr oh kah-fay)*—éclair filled with coffee-flavored cream

éclair au chocolat *(ay-klehr oh sho-ko-lah)*—éclair filled with chocolate cream

en anglais *(ahn ahn-gleh)*—in English

Etats-Unis *(ay-tahz-oo-nee)*—United States

euro *(ooh-roh)*—European money

farine *(fah-reen)*—flour

fermé *(fayr-may)*—closed

flan *(flahn)*—a custard covered with caramel

framboise *(frahm-bwahz)*—raspberry

frangipane *(frahn-zhee-pahn)*—an almond-flavored cream or paste

Frère Jacques *(freh-ruh zhahk)*—Brother Jacques; a French lullaby that is often sung as a round

gargoyle *(gahr-goil)*—a carved human or animal figure projecting from the gutter of a building

génoise *(zhay-nwahz)* **cake**—an Italian sponge cake named after the city of Genoa

grand-mère *(grahn-mehr)*—grandmother

grand-père *(grahn-pehr)*—grandfather

guillotine *(ghee-yo-teen)*—a machine widely used during the French Revolution for beheading people

Île Saint-Louis *(eel san-loo-ee)*—one of two natural islands in the Seine river in Paris

J'ai faim *(zhay fehm)*—I am hungry

Je l'aime *(zhuh lem)*—I love it

je ne sais quoi *(zhun say kwah)*—a special quality that cannot be described easily

Je regrette *(zhuh ruh-gret)*—I'm sorry

Je t'aime *(zhuh tem)*—I love you

Je vais bien *(zhuh vay byehn)*—I am fine

l'Arc de Triomphe *(lark duh tree-ohmf)*—a monument in Paris that honors those who fought and died for France in the French Revolution and Napoleonic wars

la glace *(lah glahss)*—ice cream

la Marseillaise *(lah mahr-say-yez)*—France's national anthem

la poste *(lah pohst)*—post office; label on public mailbox

la prise de la Bastille *(lah preez duh luh bah-stee-yuh)*—Bastille Day, or France's independence day, celebrated on July 14

le goûter *(luh goo-tay)*—afternoon snack

le Louvre *(luh loo-vruh)*—one of the world's largest museums and a central landmark of Paris le Sacré-Coeur *(luh sah-kreh kur)*—a famous stone church called "the Sacred Heart of Montmartre"

les filles *(lay feess)*—girls

les Halles *(lay ahl)*—a neighborhood in Paris famous for its baking and cooking shops

les jardins du Luxembourg *(lay zhahr-dehn dyew lewks-em-boorg)*—Luxembourg Gardens, the second-largest public park in Paris

macaron *(mah-kah-rohn)*—a double-layer round cookie that comes in all kinds of colors and flavors

madame *(mah-dahm)*—Mrs., ma'am

madeleine *(mahd-lehn)*—a small, rich cake baked in a shell-shaped mold

mademoiselle *(mahd-mwah-zel)*—Miss, young lady

maman *(mah-mahn)*—mother, mama

Marchons! *(mahr-shohn)*—Let's march!

marionettes *(mahr-yoh-net)*—puppets

merci *(mehr-see)*—thank you

merci beaucoup *(mehr-see boh-koo)*—thank you very much

meringue *(muh-rehng)*—a light mixture of egg whites and sugar that is baked and used to top pies and cakes

millefeuille *(meel-foy)*—a layered pastry with a glazed top of swirled chocolate and vanilla icing

moi aussi *(mwah oh-see)*—me too

monsieur *(muh-syuh)*—Mister, sir

Montmartre *(mohn-mahr-truh)*—a hill in the north of Paris and the district that surrounds it

Napoléon *(nah-poh-lay-ohn)*—the ruler of France after the French Revolution; also another name for *millefeuille*

noisette *(nwah-zet)*—hazelnut

non *(nohn)*—no

Nos mères sont soeurs *(noh mehr sohn sur)*—Our mothers are sisters

Notre Dame *(noh-truh dahm)*—a Catholic cathedral in Paris; one of the largest, most famous churches in the world

oui *(wee)*—yes

pains au chocolat *(pen oh shoh-koh-lah)*—chocolate croissants

pains aux raisins *(pen oh ray-zan)*—raisin bread

Parlez-vous anglais? *(pahr-lay voo ahn-gleh)*—Do you speak English?

pâtisserie *(pah-tee-suh-ree)*—a French bakery that specializes in pastries and desserts

petite chienne *(puh-teet shyen)*—little dog (female)

petite pâtisserie *(puh-teet pah-tee-suh-ree)*—little bakery

pharmacie *(fahr-mah-see)*—pharmacy or drugstore

Pont des Arts *(pohn dayz ahr)*—The Arts Bridge, which crosses the Seine; tourists attach padlocks to it as a symbol of love

pourquoi *(poor-kwah)*—why

quai *(keh)*—river walk

Quel beau bébé! *(kel boh bay-bay)*—What a beautiful baby!

Qu'est-ce que c'est? *(kess kuh say)*—What is this?

qui *(kee)*—who

quiche *(keesh)*—an open-faced custard pie made with eggs, milk, cheese, and vegetables or meat

quoi *(kwah)*—what

ragoût de lapin *(rah-goo duh luh-pehn)*—rabbit stew

Recommence! *(ruh-koh-mahnss)*—Begin again!

rue *(rew)*—street

Seine *(sehn)*—a nearly 500-mile-long river that flows through Paris and into the English Channel

sel *(sel)*—salt

s'il te plaît *(seel tuh pleh)*—please; used with family and friends

s'il vous plaît *(seel voo pleh)*—please; used with people you don't know well

Sonnez les matines *(soh-nay lay mah-teen)*—Morning bells are ringing

sortie *(sor-tee)*—exit

spatule en bois *(spah-tewl ahn bwah)*—a wooden spoon

sucre *(soo-kruh)*—sugar

tablier du jour *(tah-blee-ay dyew zhoor)*—apron of the day

tarte *(tahrt)*—a pastry shell filled with fruit or custard

travail *(trah-vahy)*—work

très difficile *(treh dee-fee-seel)*—very difficult

truffle *(troo-fluh)*—a soft chocolate candy covered with cocoa or chopped nuts

tuiles *(tweel)*—flat rectangular cookies or "tiles" that are set to cool over a curved surface

Tu t'appelles *(tew tah-pel)*—Your name is . . .

une arbre *(ewn ar-bruh)*—a tree

une cul de poule *(ewn kuy duh pool)*—a bowl

un peu *(uhn puh)*—a little

un platane *(uhn plah-tahn)*—a sycamore (tree)

Versailles *(vehr-sahy)*—King Louis XIV's main palace; also the French town where it is located

Veux-tu *(vuh-tew)*—Do you want . . .

Veux-tu manger? *(vuh-tew mahn-zhay)*—Do you want to eat?

voilà *(vwah-lah)*—here it is, or there it is

About the Author

Mary Casanova is always full of ideas. The author of over 30 books—including *Cécile: Gates of Gold*, *Jess*, *Chrissa*, *Chrissa Stands Strong*, *McKenna*, and *McKenna, Ready to Fly!*—she often travels as far away as Norway, Belize, and France for research.

For *Grace*, she returned to Paris—this time with her grown daughter, Kate—where they biked, explored, and took a French baking class together. Mary comes from a long line of bakers. Her grandmothers baked fragrant breads; her mother made the "world's best" caramel rolls and cinnamon rolls; and Mary, too, loves baking breads, cakes, and cookies.

When she's not writing—or traveling for research or to speak at schools and conferences—she's likely reading a good book, horseback riding in the northwoods of Minnesota, or hiking with her husband and three dogs.